DOGHOUSE ROSES

◆ ◆ ◆ ◆ ◆ ◆ ◆ ◆ ◆ ◆ ◆ ◆ ◆ ◆ ◆ ◆ ◆ ◆ ◆

STORIES

STEVE EARLE

A MARINER BOOK

HOUGHTON MIFFLIN COMPANY

BOSTON ◆ NEW YORK

First Mariner Books edition 2002

For information about permission to reproduce selections
from this book, write to Permissions, Houghton Mifflin Company,
215 Park Avenue South, New York, New York 10003.

Visit our Web site: www.houghtonmifflinbooks.com.

Library of Congress Cataloging-in-Publication Data
Earle, Steve.
Doghouse roses : stories / Steve Earle.
    p.   cm.
Contents: Doghouse roses — Wheeler County — Jaguar dance —
Taneytown — Billy the Kid — The Internationale — The red
suitcase — A eulogy of sorts — The reunion — The witness —
A well-tempered heart.
ISBN 0-618-04026-9
ISBN 0-618-21924-2 (pbk.)
    1. United States — Social life and customs — 20th century —
Fiction.
PS3555.A6825 D64 2001
813'.54—DC21   00-068247

Book design by Robert Overholtzer

Printed in the United States of America

DOC 10 9 8 7 6 5 4 3

AUTHOR'S NOTE: I apologize in advance to anyone I may have
unintentionally offended either by neglecting them in the
acknowledgments or by including them in the fiction that follows.

DOGHOUSE ROSES

FOR MY MOTHER,

Barbara Thomas Earle,

who introduced me

to words

◆

Acknowledgments

Thanks to Alice Randall for believing in me and sending my stories (without my permission) to Anton Mueller, my incredibly supportive editor at Houghton Mifflin; Mark Jacobson, Nancy Cardozo, and Terry Bisson, my New York literary support group; Tony Fitzpatrick, painter, draftsman, printer, poet, actor, amigo, hero; Elisa Sanders for keeping up with all the bits and pieces; Dan Gillis for communicating with Anton when we weren't speaking; Rosemary Carroll for doing the deal and telling me I was "a good writer" when I needed to hear it; Danny Goldberg for his continued encouragement and patronage. And to Sara for being Sara.

Contents

DOGHOUSE ROSES

DOGHOUSE ROSES

PICK ANY MEANS of transportation, public or private, over land, sea, or air. No matter which direction you travel, it takes three hours to get out of L.A. Yeah, I know there are all those folks with a head start for the Grapevine out in Northridge and Tarzana, but hell, to those of us in the trenches, the real Angelenos, those places are only luminescent names on big green signs seemingly suspended in midair above the 101 Freeway. Yeah, yeah, I know all about the good citizens of Encino and Toluca Lake who are always bragging about the convenience of friendly little Burbank Airport, but let's get real — they're not going anywhere anyway.

I'm talking about the other side of the hill — Downtown, Hollywood, Santa Monica, Venice, and Silver Lake — the transient heart of the city, the L.A. of Raymond Chandler, Chet Baker, and Tom Waits. A place where folks come to do Great Things — make movies and records, write screenplays and novels, which they hope will become screenplays someday, because that's where the money is. And every-fucking-body's got a "treatment" that they're working on, including half of the L.A.P.D. Most of these folks only wind up as minor characters in the work of the fortunate few. You've seen them — aging bit players with tough, brown hides, mummified from years of sitting around motel swimming pools waiting for the phone to ring. The drug-ravaged former rock stars in raggedy-ass Porches and Saabs on an unending orbit of the downtown streets. Even the lucky ones only get as far as the Hollywood Hills or maybe Malibu, where they live out their lives with their backs to the world's widest and deepest ocean, waiting for wildfire to rain down from the canyons above. And should they decide to get out? Well, like I said, it takes three hours, and most people simply don't have the resolve.

Bobby Charles certainly didn't. He left L.A. in disgrace, low-riding in the passenger seat of his soon-to-be ex-wife's BMW. Not that he wanted to go, but this town kicked his ass so thoroughly there was simply no fight left in him. Kim West (she had never taken Bobby's last name, for professional reasons) had finally given up on her talented but troubled husband of five years, and now she just wanted him out of her town.

When Kim and Bobby met, he was a country-rock singer whose first marriage had already begun to buckle under the stress of constant touring, the distance alone taking a considerable toll. His wife and two kids were back in Nashville, but his real home was a forty-foot Eagle bus he shared with his band and crew. At age thirty-five Bobby was somewhat of a cult figure, the kind of recording artist who, thanks to a loyal following, sold one hundred thousand records per release, although this was barely enough to recoup his recording costs. The critics loved his work, however, and he lent a certain amount of integrity to a record label's roster. Before Kim came along, he had always considered L.A. a nice place to visit, at best.

Bobby had always avoided strong women like the plague, but something about the diminutive, up-and-coming producer fascinated him. Kim came out from St. Louis to attend the UCLA film school, switching to a business major midway through her second year. She went on to an M.B.A. and a job at a major studio. When a mutual friend introduced the pair at a party after the Grammy Awards, Kim thought Bobby was cute, in a primitive sort of way, like Crocodile Dundee or something. She was bored to tears with dating other "industry" types, who saved all the receipts from dinner and talked shop in bed. Bobby was a little loud, a little reckless, and she knew her mother would hate him.

They left the party together in a rented 5.0 Mustang convertible. They wound up parked somewhere way up Mulholland Drive with Kim's panties hanging on the rearview mirror, breathlessly gazing down on all those lights. From that moment, L.A. had Bobby Charles by the balls.

Bobby didn't discover heroin in L.A. Hell, he grew up in San Antonio, Texas, 150 miles from the Mexican border. Despite the much publicized efforts of the U.S. government, brown heroin steadily seeped across the Rio Grande like tainted blood from a gangrenous wound. Bobby first tried it at an impromptu party at a friend's house when he was fourteen. For years he managed to get away with his off-and-on habit. He always managed to detox in time for this tour or that record, and even if he was dope-sick he never missed a show. By the time he met Kim, though, it was starting to catch up with him. Once Bobby left his family and moved to L.A., cheap, strong dope, guilt, and a long, nasty divorce combined to provide him with all the excuse any addict needs to bottom out.

At first it was just a matter of L.A.'s dependable supply of heroin, but pretty soon Bobby discovered speedballs — deadly intravenous cocktails of heroin and cocaine. It wasn't long before he had two habits to support. In L.A. time passes in its own surreal fashion — too subtle to even be detectable to folks who are used to four seasons. So if you asked Bobby, he couldn't tell you exactly when his habit got to be too much work. He only knew that at some point, in what passed for a moment of clarity, he enrolled in a private methadone program. He woke up early every morning to line up at the clinic with the other "clients" to take communion at the little window — a plastic cup of the bitter powder dissolved in an orange-flavored liquid, chased by water from the cooler. Bobby was then "free" from the need to run down to Hoover Street to buy heroin twice a day. So he took up smoking crack.

Because he no longer used needles, Bobby told himself and anyone who would listen that he was back on track. He'd get smoked up and rattle on for hours about the "next record." Kim listened dutifully, but she knew it was only talk. Bobby hadn't written a song in more than three years. How could he? All of his guitars (along with a few that didn't belong to him) were in the pawnshop.

Kim knew Bobby was a junkie when she married him. She just didn't know he was a *junkie* junkie. At first she saw dope as part of Bobby's "thing," his mystique. It made him seem more dangerous, and after all, she was slumming. It stopped being cute when money began to turn up missing from her account. Or when he called her at work, whacked out of his skull and thoroughly convinced that their little craftsman bungalow in Larchmont Village was surrounded by police. Kim, having little or no experience in such matters, immediately called her lawyer and rushed home to find Bobby hiding in the hall closet with a loaded shotgun and a crack pipe. When she opened the door and stood there in tears, Bobby only stared back indignantly.

"What?"

That was the day that Kim decided to bail, but she couldn't bring herself to simply leave. After all, she really loved the guy;

she was just at the end of her rope. She decided that if she could just get Bobby out of L.A., back to Nashville where his friends were, or maybe just as far as Texas where his folks lived, maybe — well, at least she wouldn't have to watch him die.

So Kim went to Jeff Shapiro, her boss at the studio, and asked for a leave of absence, which under the circumstances he was more than willing to grant. Shapiro always considered Bobby a hick and beneath Kim anyway. So Kim then canceled her subscription to the *Los Angeles Times*, notified the home security service that she and Bobby would be out of town indefinitely, serviced the car, and picked up some cash at the bank on the way home.

Bobby never knew what hit him. It took Kim less than half an hour to pack some T-shirts and the few pairs of jeans that still fit Bobby (he'd lost an alarming amount of weight) and a few changes of clothes for herself. She told him it would do them both good to get away for a while. Bobby went through the motions of putting up a fight, but before he knew it he was in the car headed down Beverly Boulevard toward the 101.

They didn't get far. Junkies can't go directly from point A to point B like other people, mainly because another hit always lies somewhere in between. First they stopped at the methadone clinic on Beverly and picked up Bobby's daily dose and a week's worth of "take-homes" for the road. Kim had already called the doctor in advance and begged for these, because doses "to go" were a privilege and Bobby hadn't been able to manage a single "clean" urine specimen in six months on the program.

Between the clinic and the freeway, tucked in between the innocuous little bungalows, were at least fifty corners where street kids and soda pop gangsters sold crack cocaine (called "rock" on the West Coast) to the drive-up trade. Kim and Bobby made it as far as the left turn onto Vermont Avenue, just before the 101 on-ramp, then Bobby threatened to get out of the car if Kim didn't drive him to a nearby spot. Reluctantly, she agreed, telling herself that this would be the last time.

They headed north on Vermont and took a right into a little rundown corner of East Hollywood. Two more rights followed by a quick left brought Bobby and his reluctant chauffeur to a cul-de-sac, cut off from the rest of the world by the freeway viaduct — a great graffiti-covered concrete monstrosity that bore the rest of the world noisily over the heads of the folks who had to live in this desperate little neighborhood. It was after dark, so anybody out on the street was either selling rock or "plugs" — little pieces of soap carved up to look like the real thing. Bobby was no stranger to this neighborhood. He ignored the hucksters and had Kim drag the block slowly until he spotted Luis.

"There he is."

Bobby rolled down the window and whistled; a skinny kid with Mayan features — long, sloping forehead, almond-shaped eyes, and angular nose — came running over to the car. He was all of fifteen years old.

"Hey, vato! Where you been, homes?"

Luis wasn't Bobby's only source, merely the nearest to the freeway.

"Around. What's up?"

"I got the *grandes*, homes. The monkey nuts. Check it out." Luis reached down into his sock and produced a large prescription medicine bottle, half full of off-white chunks of cooked-up coke, rattling them around like the pebbles inside a pair of maracas. Bobby noticed that Luis was acting strange, a little more wary than usual. He kept glancing nervously, from side to side, over his shoulder as they talked through the passenger-side window of Kim's BMW.

"What's up, kid? Five-O been through?"

"Naw, just some guys. Don't worry 'bout it, homes. What you need?"

"How much for all of it?"

Luis looked down at the bottle, rattled it some more, as if he was weighing it and doing the math in his head at a pace that belied his sixth-grade education.

"How 'bout two yards?"

"Come on with it." Bobby handed Luis a wad of twenties, took the bottle, and turned to Kim. "Let's roll."

They made a U-turn in the cul-de-sac and headed back toward Vermont and the 101. Kim couldn't wait to get out of the neighborhood, and Bobby had to tell her to slow down a little. About halfway up the street they met a customized Chevy van rolling toward the cul-de-sac with its lights off and the sliding cargo door locked open. Bobby looked in his side mirror just in time to see little Luis break and run as the van's headlights suddenly came on, freezing Luis in the middle of the street. Kim jumped as the van came alive with gunfire, the muzzle flash of at least three weapons visible through the open door. The last time Bobby saw Luis, he was lying face down in the street as the van circled like a great, hulking predator over a fresh kill — then it sped off, passing Kim and Bobby as if they weren't even there.

Kim drove on, her heart pounding in her throat while Bobby navigated.

"Next right. Now left. OK, one more left and we're out of Indian Country."

Kim turned left back onto Vermont. When she stopped at the light before the 101 on-ramp, she looked over at Bobby for the first time during the ordeal. He was cutting up one of the big rocks with his Buck knife, using the leather-covered console for a cutting board. His own car had hundreds of tiny slices in the upholstery by the time the police confiscated it last fall. Kim started to say something but caught herself. *Why bother? This is the last time. I'll just have it re-covered and it'll be just like new. Jesus fucking Christ, I just witnessed a murder! A fucking murder! OK, it's over. Just drive.*

She turned left across traffic and onto the 101 headed east.

"Get all the way over to the left lane, unless you want to end up in Downey or someplace."

She complied, but it irritated her to take directions from someone who had lived in L.A. all of two years. *How does he know these places?* But she knew the answer. Bobby could show locals parts of this town they never knew existed. Dope does that. It creates its own parallel geography, dark, scary places hidden from the real world behind a facade of palm trees and stucco. If you aren't looking, you won't see it — and you probably don't need to. Most of the folks on the freeway that night were simply following well-worn grooves in the asphalt to and from work or school or wherever. They only knew where to get on the freeway and where to get off. They had no idea where they really were, what kind of places and lives they were passing through or over.

Bobby did. It was an obsession with him. He roamed the freeways at night, exiting here and there just for the hell of it, to have a look around. He could tell you about the different styles of street signs and lights in the old L.A. neighborhoods. Each neighborhood had its own look — one for Hollywood, another for the Crenshaw District, and so on. He even knew a fair amount of L.A.'s checkered history, the scandals and secrets that had shaped it. Sometimes Kim was actually jealous, as if the sprawling city was a great glittering whore with whom Bobby had been unfaithful. It never pays to know this town too well.

Bobby licked his finger so that one of the pieces of the cut-up rock would adhere to it, then he stuck it in the end of his "straight shooter," a glass tube, three inches long with a piece of copper scouring pad stuffed in one end. Street addicts prefer this type of pipe for its easy-to-conceal size. Bobby liked it because he could drive and smoke without being too obvious. He turned up the flame on his disposable lighter and the rock crackled and sputtered as it melted into the copper. He inhaled slowly, deeply, and then expelled the dense white smoke out through his nose in a sort of visible and audible sigh. Kim fought back a gag, more of a Pavlovian reaction than anything else, but she just cracked her window and said nothing. In fact, nobody said anything for what seemed like an eternity. In real time only about fifteen minutes had elapsed, just about the time it took to reach the 10, before Kim had to ask, "So what the fuck was that all about?"

Bobby was suddenly forced to deal with the image of Luis, lying in the dead-end street. "I don't know. I guess he owed them money or somethin'."

Bobby's matter-of-factness bothered Kim more than anything else. His tone suggested he'd seen things like this before, which made her more than a little uncomfortable.

Bobby put another piece of rock on his pipe and hit it again. "Drag. He was a good kid. Hey, get off at the next exit. I need some smokes."

Kim complied, bitching just a little under her breath. This was their second stop and they weren't even close to being out of L.A. yet. She pulled into a 7-Eleven. Bobby hopped out, stopping halfway to the door and coming around to her side of the car.

"Need anything?"

She shook her head, mildly irritated at the afterthought. Then again, when she had stopped at the grocery store that afternoon to buy all the stuff she needed for the road — gum, cigarettes, and such — it never occurred to her to pick up a carton for Bobby. She watched him through the glass wall of the convenience store, standing in line with an armload of junk food. It wasn't long ago that she would have done anything for Bobby. She packed his bags when he went on the road, shopped for his clothes, even cooked occasionally, something she'd never done for anyone, including herself. Their house was filled with gifts she had bought for his birthday, Christmas, Father's Day, anniversaries, along with some she bought for no specific occasion. There were maps (one of Bobby's passions before he lost interest in everything but dope), books, guitars, computers, and recording equipment — most of which was in the pawnshop now. Bobby bought her stuff too — jewelry, art, even the BMW that now carried him from town — but Kim's favorite gifts were the roses.

Doghouse roses, Bobby called them. You know. Those single roses they sell at the checkout in convenience stores. They come wrapped in cellophane, with the little plastic bulb of water at the base of the stem. Men buy them for their significant others when they stay out too late or forget an anniversary or a birthday. Bobby bought literally hundreds of them over the years, as he limped home from one misadventure or another, and Kim had saved every one. They were all over the house, pressed between the pages of every big book — Bibles, atlases, dictionaries. She had often asked herself, Why? Each rose represented a disappointment, a broken promise, and a sleep-less night. Why commemorate them? The passenger-side door suddenly opened and Bobby plopped down next to her with a sack full of provisions. Sticking out of the top, in between a motorcycle magazine and a Slim Jim, was a yellow rose.

Kim burst into tears. She was still recovering from the inci-dent in the cul-de-sac, and the very idea of another rose was a little more than she could take. To make matters worse, Bobby offered the gift as a child would, trusting the flower to some-how intercede on his behalf and make everything all right.

And maybe it was a child she saw when she finally reached out and accepted the rose, wrapping her arms around Bobby and cradling his head against her breast. Her soft reassuring tone and the words that came out of her mouth seemed al-most comically mismatched. "Goddamn, baby. We could have been killed back there."

Bobby said nothing. He knew she was right, and he already felt the familiar first pangs of guilt. It took a lot of dope just to overcome the ever-increasing weight of the accumulated guilt he dragged with him through every single day. Guilt had be-come second nature to him. He was guilty of leaving his fam-ily. He was guilty of letting down his band and his fans. He was guilty of subjecting Kim to all of his junkie shit.

But all that would have to wait because right now, being held close and cursed at in near whispers, like a kid who had just narrowly escaped being hit by a speeding car, was as good as it got for Bobby. There was a time when this moment would have ended in the nearest motel or the back seat of the car, with the smell of sex and the relief of forgiveness in the air. And for a little while, Bobby would behave more like an adult and Kim less like a mother, and new plans and promises were made. Neither Bobby nor Kim minded that most of these were never kept. It was the illusion of healing that they lived for, the precious few breathless intervals after they made love when they weren't at cross-purposes.

No, no, no. Not this time. Kim suddenly summoned up all of her will and simply stopped crying, dabbing the mascara from her face and, less successfully, from Bobby's white T-shirt with tissue from the BMW's convenient dispenser. Bobby, electing not to push his luck, opened a twenty-ounce Dr. Pepper and lit a Marlboro. His eyes fixed on a point somewhere beyond the windshield, visible only from his perspective. His voice cracked a little as he spoke.

"I love you."

Kim carefully placed the rose on the dashboard, like an offering to whatever god governed dysfunctional relationships.

"I love you, too."

She backed out of the parking space and headed for the feeder road.

By now it's after eleven and the traffic is light, by L.A. standards. It's one of those spooky nights, entirely too quiet for a city of nine million, when mercury vapor lights throw ghostly shadows on the ground fog and the car exhaust, creating an eerie yellow glow. Spectral palm trees, their roots shackled by acres of concrete, seem to stand on tiptoes straining to keep their heads above the noxious layer at street level. The names on the big green highway signs appear suddenly and slightly out of focus — Covina, Pomona, Ontario, and on and on, and looking up through the sunroof, there still aren't any stars. Only a sort of fallout created by man-made light impacting the opaque canopy above and shattering, diffusing into colors not found in nature before falling back to earth in defeat. L.A. is one big motherfucker. Most would-be escapees become overwhelmed with the immensity of the task and turn around, but not Kim. She just kept driving on — past Riverside, past Redlands — until she could feel the momentum building, as if they were finally escaping the city's considerable gravity.

Kim loved to drive and she loved her car. Bobby had given it to her for her birthday. After receiving a large advance from his publisher, he just walked into the BMW dealer and wrote a personal check for $58,000. Then he parked it in Kim's space at the studio with a big red bow taped to the grill. The car, bred for the autobahn, had seldom been turned loose on the highway, and Kim could feel the powerful engine writhe under the hood when she stepped on the accelerator. She asked Bobby to light her a cigarette and he did, firing up another for himself at the same time. For a while she actually forgot why they were on the road that night. Remembering how much she loved the car reminded her of how much she had once loved Bobby, which made her more than a little uncomfortable — but not for long. About the time they blew by San Bernardino, Bobby put another rock up on the pipe, filling the car with thick, white smoke, which reminded Kim how much she hated cocaine.

She had never had a problem coexisting with Bobby's heroin habit. Smack, by itself, made Bobby relaxed and talkative, not to mention affectionate. As long as he had heroin, he stayed home, going out only long enough to cop. Somehow unable to hold her husband responsible for his actions, Kim blamed cocaine, and she loathed it with every cell in her body. She wasn't alone. Even the L.A.P.D. agreed with her. Heroin didn't seem to breed the level of violence that permeated the more competitive coke trade. Coke addicts were edgier, more dangerous, and the young criminals that trafficked in it were colder and harder. Forget about little Luis. He was just a runner. I'm talking about the cats in the van. Crack, cocaine's cheap, smokable form, was big business and it was taking the streets by storm. People were willing to kill or be killed for the right street corner. The cops were so busy dealing with the new menace that the older, more levelheaded heroin dealers were enjoying a period of relative peace. Driving through the heroin spots was almost like a visit to the corner liquor store. Kim would even ride along sometimes, making small talk with the spot boss while Bobby transacted business at the other window.

Then one morning Bobby was at a friend's house getting high while Kim was at work. Somebody suggested running to a nearby spot for a rock. Bobby had always turned up his nose at crack, but for some reason he decided one hit couldn't hurt.

Bobby began staying awake for days at a time, ripping and running from the bank to the spot, back to the house, to the pawnshop, and back to the spot again. Kim didn't know the details, but she knew something was wrong. She began to worry enough to consult a friend who was in recovery. He suggested an intervention, but Kim couldn't go through with it. She felt like that would be a betrayal. Eventually she simply began to shut down. To slowly but surely stop loving Bobby, in self-defense.

Interstate 10 stretched out in a great black ribbon trimmed in iridescent white, pulling the BMW along through the night as it threaded through the hills toward the high desert ahead. The air began to gradually clear as they climbed, and Kim rolled down the windows and opened the sunroof, purging the crack smoke from the car. *Just keep driving.* The lights of Palm Springs appeared off to their right, twinkling through the heat waves. The sign said "BANNING/MORONGO INDIAN RES. —

NEXT EXIT." *Now we're getting somewhere.* Then Bobby shattered the groove.

"Baby, let's run out to Joshua Tree."

"Goddamn it, Bobby, no. No fucking way. We're almost out of here, please!"

But she knew that that's exactly where they would go.

Joshua Tree National Park lies 140 miles east of downtown L.A., 794,000 acres straddling the high Mojave and the lower Colorado deserts. Named for the large multibranched cacti that dominate its landscape, the park is bordered by Interstate 10 on the southwest, just as the "southern route" back east makes its last dash for the Arizona border. The Mojave half of the park, ranging from about 3,000 to 5,200 feet at the top of Quail Mountain, is one of the most beautiful places on earth by anyone's standards. But to Bobby Charles, it was sacred.

Not that Bobby was particularly outdoorsy or anything. If anything he was entirely too comfortable with big cities. When he was a kid back in Texas, he hunted and fished with his dad. But as soon as he picked up the guitar, everything else took a back seat. Music was such a powerful force in his life that even heroin couldn't compete, at first. Music kept him constantly moving, first to Houston, and then back and forth across the country, finally landing him in Nashville three months short of his twentieth birthday. Bobby's first addiction was motion itself. He fell in love and got married, but he never settled down, growing more restless with every day he spent within the confines of Nashville's city limits. "High Lonesome" he called the affliction, after the heart-rending tenor of Bill Monroe. Music allowed him to escape to the road, returning to Nashville only long enough to make records and father children. The big Eagle bus carried him to places like New York, New Orleans, Chicago, or back to Texas to show off for the home folks. Bobby would play poker and watch movies with the band until they drifted, one by one, off to their bunks. Then he'd ride in the jumpseat, up front with the driver, watching the Eagle suck asphalt up under its wheels, spewing it out the back in the form of distance. When the sun came up he'd retreat to the stateroom in the back and sleep like a baby, lulled by the low, throaty hum of the big diesel only inches below his bunk. A growing following overseas allowed him to see London, Amsterdam, Dublin, even Sydney, Tokyo, and Hong Kong. Bobby got to know some of those cities intimately, but more and more he was most comfortable in the more ambiguous space between destinations — the road itself.

When Bobby moved to L.A. to live with Kim, he was in love with a beautiful, fascinating woman as well as infatuated with his new surroundings and life was good. He spent his days getting high and exploring, getting the lay of the land. One day he took a ride out to the desert on his motorcycle while Kim was at work. He was on a pilgrimage of sorts, in search of the Joshua Tree Inn. The tiny motel, on Highway 62 along the park's northern border, was a holy place in country-rock circles because Gram Parsons, credited by many with founding the movement, died there. The talented singer and songwriter had used the place as a desert hideout for several years, even extracting a promise from his road manager to cremate his body somewhere in the Joshua Tree country when his time came. When Gram expired in Room 8 from a little too much of everything one cool clear desert night in 1973, his compatriot kept his promise, stealing Gram's body from a loading dock at the L.A. airport and spiriting it away to the desert in a borrowed hearse. He then burned the body, for which he was later prosecuted and fined. Musicians in Bobby's circles prized this story, telling and retelling it whenever they met on the road, weaving it in with the songs Gram left behind and eventually creating a legend.

On his first trip to the desert, Bobby had hoped to spend the night in the inn, but by 1990 it had been converted into a home for autistic children, so he bought camping gear for his more and more frequent trips to the desert. At first Kim would go with him, and it became their weekend getaway. They'd ride in the park on Bobby's bike, Kim in back hanging on for dear life, her arms wrapped tightly around Bobby's waist. Bobby ran the bike hard because the tighter she clung to him the better he liked it. When the moon was full, the desert seemed to emit a light of its own from every rock and plant, the only dark spots being the man-made surfaces, asphalt and pitch. They'd ride well past dark. When they finally made camp, they would lie on their backs on air mattresses for hours and marvel at how close the stars seemed. Bobby would point out the planets and constellations and nebulae visible through his binoculars. Sometimes they made love under all those stars, never even bothering to pitch the fancy tent strapped to the back of the bike. They'd wake before sunrise when the desert received its meager ration of moisture in the form of a heavy dew, leaving their hair damp and driving them, shivering, deeper into Bobby's sleeping bag. Then the sun would come up, bounding over the mountains, and they'd wake suddenly to find the sleeping bag soaked nearly through from the inside out with their own sweat.

After a while Kim stopped making the trips out to the desert. She got busier at the studio making movies, and Bobby got busier on the streets, slowly killing himself. Once again he set himself in motion, albeit in circles, breaking out of his rapidly deteriorating orbit only when High Lonesome caught up with him and drove him east, into the desert. The Joshua Tree trips became his only respite from the junkie grind; only now, they were desperate, lonely sojourns. Eventually he was incapable of riding a motorcycle, or camping for that matter, so he would drive aimlessly in and around the park, sleeping in his car by the roadside if at all. Sometimes he would run out of coke and drive back to L.A. to cop. After purchasing what he needed, he'd turn around and head right back to the desert, sometimes passing within a mile of his house on the way to the freeway. On three occasions he fell asleep at the wheel, totaling three different vehicles — two of his own and one rental — but by some miracle he walked away from each accident with only cuts and bruises.

Somebody was trying to tell Bobby Charles something, but he wasn't listening. Friends and family back in Texas and Tennessee had all but given up on ever reaching him again. They heard the rumors that filtered back from the coast, and the news was never good. Bobby's L.A. friends saw him almost as infrequently and usually only as he passed them going the other direction on a busy Hollywood street, oblivious to everyone and everything around him.

Only Kim could occasionally penetrate the cone of silence that surrounded him, and even her voice grew fainter everyday. In time Kim simply stopped trying, but Bobby didn't notice. By then he heard only the din of his own spirit dying, slowly and painfully. As usual, Bobby looked to the desert for answers. Somehow he felt that something out there could purge him of a life's collection of demons and leave them exposed and impotent writhing on the sand. Exposed to the merciless high desert sun and miles from any suitable human host, the wretched beasts would evaporate once and for all and trouble the world no more. What's more, he knew there were worse fates. Contrary to the dogma of faith, however well intended, he knew the spirit doesn't always outlive the flesh. He saw them every day, broken bodies with sunken chests rattling around the streets like animated skeletons. Bobby faced his own worst fears there, dimly reflected in lifeless eyes. Eventually he stopped going to the desert, or anywhere else for that matter. He suspended all pretense of taking care of himself, going for days without showering and living on a steady diet of ice cream and Dr. Pepper. He only left the house to cop, driving straight home and sitting in the tiny half bath in the hallway for hours with his pipe. He refused to answer the telephone or even play back his messages, and after a while no one called anyway. At the end of a two-year battle for the soul of one Bobby Charles, desert vs. city, L.A. had won, hands down.

"Let's run out to Joshua Tree."

At some point during the fight that ended, as usual, when Kim's will finally conformed to Bobby's, they blew right by Highway 62, their customary route to the park's north entrance at Twentynine Palms. The southern entrance remained, the back door, about sixty miles down the interstate. Bobby had never been that way before, but that sort of thing never bothered him. He sat up straight in his seat on the passenger side of the Beamer, alert for the first time since they left Hollywood, again giving Kim directions. Kim fell into step like a trooper, a veteran of a thousand improvised expeditions into out-of-the-way places with Bobby at the helm. Once inside the park, no directions were necessary, for there was only one road that ran vaguely north and south, jogging to the east and west only as it wound its way through the western edge of the Eagle Mountains. It was one of those pristine desert nights that Bobby loved. The moon was full and he reached across the car to turn off the headlights, slapping playfully at Kim's hand when she tried to turn them back on. Her eyes adjusted and she found, to her surprise, that she had no trouble driving without them. The desert unfolded around them in unearthly detail, and it seemed to lift Bobby out of his fog a little. He even forgot about the pipe for a while.

"Darlin', why don't you let me drive?"

What the hell. I lost control as soon as I left the interstate. She stopped the car in the middle of the narrow blacktop road, not even bothering to pull over onto the shoulder. As she walked around to the passenger side, she brushed by Bobby going the other way, but they didn't stop or speak. They were both overcome by the profound stillness. Absolute quiet. There wasn't a car in sight in either direction. As a matter of fact, nothing was moving.

Bobby knew the desert well enough to know that there was life all around them, and that the cool of the nighttime was when they issued from their hiding places where they lay all day long conserving moisture and energy. Bobby had spent a hundred nights lying on his side in a sleeping bag, propped up on one elbow, watching Lilliputian armies of tarantulas, hundreds of them in a group, passing noiselessly in eerie procession, an arachnophobe's worst nightmare. There were scorpions hunting by the light of the outsized desert moon, hurrying here and there, desperate to find a meal before the unforgiving Mojave drove them back to lightless asylum beneath a rock or the roots of a creosote bush. Sometimes the larger creatures, the bobcat, coyote, and kit fox, seemed just as out of place as the humans who visited, transient somehow, preying mostly on the lowly kangaroo rat who seemed to be food for everyone above his station, including the owls who were masters of the dry night air.

Tonight, however, was different. It was as if the desert itself was sizing up the intruders, weighing their intentions before giving the all clear to the myriad of creatures and elements under its protection.

Bobby slid behind the wheel and fumbled around until he found the lever, releasing the seat to travel backward on its track as far as it would go. Leaving the lights off, he set the car in motion down the black asphalt, deeper into the desert, further out of control. Kim was starting to relax a little. She had always depended on Bobby to bring her to the desert or any other out-of-the-way place, and she was conditioned to surrender control in such situations. It simply wasn't in her nature to stray from the beaten path on her own.

Bobby was dependent on Kim as well. He needed her approval. He genuinely didn't give a damn what the rest of the world thought, but Kim was his weakness. He wanted desperately to please her, even impress her, but he could not endure her disapproval. Ironically, Bobby's couldn't-give-a-fuck swagger was the first thing that attracted Kim to him, and now that he depended on her for anything, she disrespected him for it. But she couldn't stop taking care of him, cleaning up after him, and bailing him out.

Suddenly Bobby saw a sign on the left, the small, rustic type favored by the National Park Service. It said KEY'S VIEW 15. He took the left, two wheels crunching on the gravel shoulder, and headed west so the moon was behind him now and dominating his mirrors, white and almost blinding. The road gradually traversed the length of a long ridge, eventually carrying them to the highest point in the park, where the road dead-ended in a cul-de-sac.

Kim started laughing out loud. "This must be my night for dead-ends."

Bobby wasn't listening. He threw open the car door and climbed out, slipping a little on the loose gravel. He staggered slightly as he made his way to the overlook. The desert stretched out before him like a diorama in a museum. The moon behind him provided the light, but it appeared to emanate from below, from the desert itself. The lights of Palm Springs backlit the Santa Rosa Mountains to his left. Suddenly Bobby threw his head back until it rested between his shoulder blades; his arms stretched wide, his silhouette wraithlike against the sky. From where she sat in the car, Kim thought he was looking up at the sky, drinking in the moonlight and all those stars. It wasn't until she opened her door that she realized he was crying, almost keening like some mythic death messenger, the wails punctuated by deep, gasping body-wrenching sobs.

Kim didn't hesitate. She went to him straight away, stopping only to grab a blanket from the back seat. She draped it over his shoulders, pulling him closer as he collapsed to his knees, burying his face at her waist as she wrapped the blanket around them both and held him until the last sob subsided. She knew what was next. She knew as soon as she had opened the door and heard Bobby crying. No amount of will could stop it. They made love with only the blanket between them and the cold, hard ground, and it was exquisitely painful like scratching a wound that hasn't quite healed. They even slept for a while, Kim pulling one corner of the blanket up over Bobby's shoulder as the desert went about its business around them. A kit fox passed by paying them little notice. A coyote approached cautiously, turning away once the human smell awakened some primordial memory. There were literally hundreds of smaller creatures through the makeshift campsite that night, some navigating around the unfamiliar obstacle, some simply scurrying up and over the pair as they slept.

As always, the intimacy created a kind of emotional amnesia. Kim woke up when she missed Bobby's warmth against her. She wrapped the blanket around herself as she sat up and called his name. When he didn't answer, she quickly dressed and walked back up the trail to the car, still under the spell of the "old Bobby" and telling herself things like *Maybe if I just hang in there a little longer.*

When she got back to the car the enchantment evaporated. Bobby sat straight up behind the wheel of the car. She called his name but he didn't answer. Her heart stopped. Kim called again. Nothing. She screamed his name at the top of her lungs, simultaneously breaking into a run, losing the struggle for traction on the loose gravel and falling badly, skinning her knee then quickly regaining her feet. Her mind raced. *Don't you die on me, Bobby Charles! Not now! Not here! Goddamn it, Bobby you sonofabitch! Just like you to pussy out on me just when things were looking good! Looking good? Where did that come from? Just like you to die out here in the middle of nowhere just like your goddamn junkie hero Gram What's-His-Name.*

By the time Kim reached the car she was a mess. Her hair hung limp in her eyes, which were swollen from crying. Her sundress was covered with sand, and blood ran in two tiny streams from the scrape on her knee. Bobby still wasn't answering. He remained motionless, his mannequinlike eyes fixed on the horizon. She tried to open the door but it was locked. She pounded on the window. No response. She pounded on the roof of the car with both fists, creating a drumlike rumble and screaming Bobby's name. She was about to look for a rock to smash the glass when the power window suddenly came to life, releasing a cloud of smoke thicker than midsummer L.A. smog. Bobby said nothing, but the look on his face told Kim that he was hearing her voice for the first time. She looked down in Bobby's lap and there, cradled almost lovingly in his right hand, was the pipe.

The rest of the trip was uneventful. They got a room in Barstow, where Kim showered and slept a few hours while Bobby smoked and stared at the TV. About dark she settled behind the wheel with a resolve she'd never known in her life. Kim pushed the BMW hard, the radar detector warning her where to take it easy, averaging ninety miles per hour for the whole trip. At a checkpoint just west of El Paso the border patrol took one look at Bobby and put a dog in the car, but the dope had run out somewhere in Arizona. By late the next night they were in Houston, having covered fourteen hundred miles in the same time it had taken them to get out of California.

Bobby's folks were glad to see him, although they were surprised that he hadn't called and concerned about his weight loss. Both Kim and Bobby put up a good front through dinner, after which Bobby asked for the car keys. Kim knew he wanted to go downtown and cop, so she made the excuse that she had to have the car serviced so they could get an early start for Tennessee in the morning. Rather than provoking a fight in his parents' home, Bobby asked his dad for his keys, saying he needed cigarettes. As soon as he was out the door, Kim excused herself and went to the guestroom and packed, leaving Bobby's things behind. When Bobby's folks asked where she was going, she said nothing, just walked faster, not stopping until she was behind the wheel and headed for the interstate.

When Bobby returned (three hours later), his parents were at a loss for an explanation. On the dresser in the guestroom was a motel stationery envelope and one red doghouse rose. Inside the envelope were twenty-five twenty-dollar bills and a note that said:

> Bobby,
> I'm going away for a while and when I get back, I'm going to file for a divorce. Please, don't try to find me. I can't do this anymore. My attorney will contact you.
>
> Kim

Not "Love, Kim" or "Fuck You" or anything, just "Kim."

So Bobby Charles completed his trip to Tennessee alone. He hung around Houston until he wore out his welcome. Then he had his publisher wire him some cash and prepay a plane ticket to Nashville, where Bobby continued to do all the right things to kill himself for three more years. Before it was over, he had nothing. No money. No car. No place to live. But the worst was yet to come. Without the insulation money and connections afforded, Bobby eventually piled up enough drug charges to draw a little jail time. After a few weeks involuntarily clean in jail, the fog cleared just a little and somehow something happened to Bobby. He decided he wanted to live. It was years later, after some clean time under his belt, before he realized that by leaving him in Houston and refusing to participate in his habit anymore, Kim had probably saved his life.

By the time he was released from jail, Bobby was writing songs again. He began to perform once in a while, taking it easy at first, until finally he resumed making critically acclaimed, moderately successful records as if nothing ever happened.

Well, almost as if nothing ever happened. Kim was all over

most of his songs. At first they were bitter and angry songs designed to wreak vengeance over the airwaves, but after a few albums venom gave way to melancholy and resignation. He never came back to L.A. again without his manager or another suitable chaperone, and he always left as soon as his business was concluded. Sometimes Bobby and Kim would run into each other when he was in town, but they never spoke, preferring to make each other uncomfortable from across the room. He never went to the desert again. Any desert. Period. And he never bought anyone roses, ever again.

WHEELER COUNTY

HARLEY WATTS looked down a long, flat stretch of Interstate 40 west of Shamrock, Texas, the way a man would size up an old acquaintance from across a crowded barroom. You know, that one ambiguous instant between the time you see them and they see you when you have to decide whether you're glad to see them or not. Actually Harley and I-40 were more than casual acquaintances.

"This is where I came in."

He realized he had spoken out loud just as the words died a quick, merciful death in the emptiness between asphalt and sky.

"Ten years." Out loud once again.

He wondered if his guitar was up to the sudden changes in temperature this journey surely held in store. The old Gibson had always passed the road test with flying colors, but that was before it spent a decade in a fairly constant climate. Hell, it spent most of the past five years in its beat-up old case under Delores's bed. Not that Harley was a great guitar player — or singer for that matter. Every song he'd ever written bore a woman's given name as its title. Some of his best efforts had been retooled more than once, each time in honor of yet another object of his attention if not his affection. So let's just say Harley was no Bob Dylan, but he may have been a Woody

Guthrie of sorts. For if Harley was wasting a god-given talent while lingering in Wheeler County, Texas, it was hitchhiking.

More than likely God never woke up and decided he was going to make himself a hitchhiker, but if he had, it would have looked a lot like Harley Watts. Five feet eleven inches, 185 pounds. Shoulder-length brown hair. Brown eyes that always seemed to squint even though he had twenty-twenty vision. Indian eyes with premature crow's-feet carved by the last rays of hundreds of sunsets. Eyes that always seemed to be focused somewhere else. Someplace beyond here. On down the road.

Ten years ago, almost to the day, a thinner, tanner Harley had stood on this very spot fresh from a four-hundred-mile ride in the back of a Chevy pickup, which was a good thing in hitchhiking terms if the weather was good. And the weather was great in the spring of 1978, somewhere out in the big-ass middle of West Texas. In fact, it had been pretty damn good since about Nashville, which meant that a pickup truck with an already occupied shotgun seat was the ultimate ride. Sun shining, wind blowing, miles rolling by at a magical clip without the distraction of feeling obligated to carry on a meaningless conversation with the operator of the vehicle du jour.

If you'd hitchhiked as many miles as Harley, you could spot a ride a hundred yards up the road. The Good Samaritan behind the wheel of a big rig is a myth. Eighteen-wheelers are too hard to stop and besides, miles are money. By the same token, the blonde in the convertible is also a fantasy, a mirage concocted in the sun-baked brain of a hapless hiker or a lie spun in a bar to impress the gullible. In the sixties any road warrior worth his salt knew Volkswagens were a hitchhiker's best friend. Most rides were long cramped ordeals, chin bare inches from your knees while your benefactor rattled on and on about the *Tibetan Book of the Dead* or something you cared even less about. By 1978, however, even the venerable VW was beginning to disappear from the nation's highways as its owners settled down, opened futon stores, had kids named Dylan and Chelsea, and bought Volvos. And Volvos almost never pick up hitchhikers.

So there he was, ten years ago, standing on the on-ramp, one foot on his guitar case, one thumb in the breeze, bound for California.

Harley had been damn near everywhere in North America since he left his hometown of Louisville, Kentucky, in 1971, including Alaska and large chunks of Canada and Mexico. He'd even seen Southeast Asia courtesy of Uncle Sam, but the one prize that eluded him was California. . . . Land of Steinbeck. Crucible of Kerouac and Cassidy. Playground of Kesey and the Pranksters. Ground Zero for the Revolution *and* the Summer of Love. But every time Harley set his sights on the mother of all destinations, something always got in the way. Sometimes it was a woman. Well, OK, most of the time. Sometimes it was the latest in a long line of "opportunities" to make a "lot" of money with a minimum of effort or, more important, little or no commitment. Sometimes winter (or summer) came early that year. Sometimes Harley would just find a spot on the planet that suited him a little better than others for the time being, and he'd just hang.

The latest obstacle to impose itself in Harley's path had been one Deputy Sheriff Arlon Ness. Arlon had spent all but four of his twenty-seven years, one year younger than Harley, right there in Shamrock. It was curiosity more than anything else that caused Arlon to stop on the overpass that morning ten years ago, just as ol' Harley stuck out that golden thumb of his. Here was an opportunity to get a good close-up look at something he'd only seen on TV, a real, live, honest-to-God vagrant. Arlon never intended to arrest Harley that afternoon. He only radioed the Wheeler County Sheriff's Department to tell Brenda, the dispatcher, about "this feller with long hair and a guitar standin' out on the off-ramp," but the sheriff happened to be standing right there in the radio room when the call came in. Sheriff Tommy Burke didn't like hippies any better in 1978 than he had in the sixties, and he grabbed the microphone from Brenda and *ordered* Arlon to "bring him in."

Harley was charged with hitchhiking on an interstate highway and vagrancy. The vagrancy charge was the part that really chapped his ass. After all, vagrancy is basically the crime of not having any money. Before Arlon came along, Harley *had* money, a little over a hundred bucks as a matter of fact. After the sheriff and the magistrate got through with him, he found himself standing in front of the county courthouse staring down in disgust at four singles and a handful of change. California never seemed farther away.

Arlon had sat across the street in his patrol car wrestling with guilt and watched as Harley fell back on a hitchhiker's last refuge — shoe leather. He struck out in long deliberate strides straight for the interstate. He didn't stop and ask for directions. He didn't have to. Knowing where the highway was at all times had become second nature to him. It was a matter of survival, an instinct like those of migratory birds. Arlon tracked Harley's every move with a level of interest he usually reserved for professional athletes or the quarter horses that run over at Ruidosa. Something deep down in Arlon's gut told him he was witnessing something special.

By the time Harley reached Fuller's Texaco, he'd built up such a head of steam that Arlon actually clocked him at just over eight miles an hour as he followed alongside in his car.

Even at that speed, with his head down, hell-bent for the interstate, Harley's built-in cop detector went off, and he suddenly stopped on the proverbial dime.

Harley had done an abrupt left face on the shoulder of the highway and was shouting at the top of his lungs. He didn't like cops in general, and *this* cop had just cost him his road stake. A hundred dollars would carry a veteran hiker like Harley halfway across the country on his own terms. Now he'd have to scramble, sleeping under bridges for lack of the price of a lousy state park camping permit. And then there was the small matter of food. So Harley just snapped. With every step he took toward Arlon's vehicle, his voice got louder and his face got redder until he was standing on the passenger side, bent over at the waist, his head and shoulders *inside* the patrol car. For the first time in his law enforcement career, Arlon Ness had his hand on his sidearm, and he was seriously considering shooting Harley Watts, but self-control won out at the last second. Arlon turned off the ignition, grabbed the keys, and bailed out of the patrol car raising both of his hands above his head, palms forward, to show Harley that he meant him no harm. For what seemed like forever, they just stood there hollering at each other across the roof of the car.

"Whoa, whoa, whoa! I just wanted to say I was *sorry!*"

Harley stopped right in the middle of a colorful dissertation on Arlon's family tree. He blinked. It was the first time a cop had ever apologized to him.

"At least let me buy you a beer."

Harley and Arlon sat facing each other at a back table in the AAA Icehouse. Actually, nobody ever called it that. The proprietor was Santiago Guitierras, the patriarch of a large fam-

ily as well as "godfather," in the old-world sense, to all of
Shamrock's relatively small Chicano community. So the locals just called it Santo's. The waitress brought the beer while
the only two Anglo customers in the joint sized each other up.
The conversation was a little slow getting started, but after
a few beers the boys discovered they had something in common.

Private Harley Watts and Second Lieutenant Arlon Ness
had each arrived in the Republic of Vietnam with their own
perspectives on the war and the world. Arlon enlisted, operating on the theory that any place would be an improvement
over Shamrock. He was twice named trainee of the month in
basic training, where he was recommended for Officer Candi-
date School. Harley, however, was drafted after losing his student deferment in the aftermath of an arrest for possessing a
minuscule amount of marijuana, and he barely managed to
stay out of the stockade during basic. Although their respective
tours of duty overlapped by some nine months, they never
met. After all, they were only two of some two-hundred-fifty
thousand troops that remained "in country" in 1971. They
returned home to entirely different situations as well. Arlon
went back to Wheeler County, where folks were generally impressed with anyone who had been anywhere. Most people in
Shamrock had come to simply ignore the seemingly endless
war on the other side of the world. Back in Louisville, though,
most of Harley's friends — that is, the ones who had managed
to stay out of the draft — were a little more judgmental. So
Harley hit the road, and Arlon went to work for the sheriff's department and got married, and neither one talked about the
war much. Even that night in Santo's, the subject merely
passed between them like a secret handshake. There was sim-

ply no reason to discuss it further, especially in public. No one else would understand anyway.

Harley let Arlon buy him several beers, the first few, because he was killing time while he formulated a new game plan; the rest, because that's just how beer is. Arlon, ever the helpful public servant and feeling even more guilty now that he discovered he actually liked Harley, suggested that he just might know a way that a man who wasn't scared of a little work might make a few bucks. The proposition of hitchhiking all the way to California on four dollars was becoming less attractive with every free beer, so Harley bought the last round while Arlon elaborated.

One of the many irons in Santo Guitierras's fire was a small construction company.

"Fair warning now, Hoss." Arlon called everybody "Hoss" after he'd had a couple of beers. "This ain't like any other construction job you ever had before. These folks work from 'can't see 'til can't see.' None of this knock off at 3:30 and go to the beer joint shit. The upside of that deal is you'll make your money back in a couple days."

So Santo was summoned to the table.

"Don Santo. Por favor."

The old man liked Arlon, mainly because he was the only gringo in Wheeler County who spoke Spanish. Besides, a man in Don Santo's position sometimes needed a friend at the sheriff's department. Even Sheriff Burke depended on their relationship whenever he had "trouble with the Meskins." Arlon introduced Harley as an "army buddy" passing through town and allowed how he would consider it a personal favor if Don Santo could throw him a few days' work. All of this was conveyed in flawless Tex-Mex.

Santo glanced briefly at Harley and then back at Arlon. "Si, no problema." Then at Harley once again. "Five-thirty in the morning. Marshall Dillon here knows where."

Five o'clock came way too early. Harley woke up on Arlon's couch with a slight hangover, sat up, and struggled to get his bearings. Arlon and his wife, Donna, lived with their three pre-school-age kids in a doublewide trailer on five and a half acres a few miles north of Shamrock. Harley could hear the couple whispering in the kitchen.

"But what if he's a psycho or something?"

"Honey, he'll hear you! What kind of talk is that anyhow? I'm a police officer for god's sake. Don't you figure I know an ax murderer when I see one? Besides, he's a vet."

None of this made Donna feel any better. Nevertheless, she packed Harley a couple of salami sandwiches and a bag of chips for lunch and handed Arlon a thermos of coffee as they hurried out the door.

The sun was just making an appearance when Arlon and Harley pulled up alongside Don Santo's old concrete-encrusted pickup. Harley gingerly climbed out of the patrol car and just stood there blinking in the half-light. It reminded Arlon of dropping a first-grader off on the first day of school.

"Go on now."

Then he backed out and headed into town to work the seven o'clock shift, leaving Harley and Santo to get acquainted.

Don Santo was a general contractor, which means he bids on any kind of construction job that comes along. More often than not, out in West Texas, far from the influence of any union, he underbid the competition. He enjoyed the advantage of a steady flow of cheap labor, mostly relatives, mostly illegal, shuttling back and forth across the border on a constant basis. Not that Santo ever exploited his workers. On the contrary, he paid much better wages than any of the Anglo employers who hired illegal aliens. He coordinated the comings and goings of various cousins and in-laws with his uncle, Eusebio, who like Santo was a man of property and a patron of his people in their hometown in Chihuahua. Between them, they decided who made the long trip north to work and who went home to Mexico for a while. It was a typically large Catholic family, so the little construction business fed well over a hundred mouths at any given time. The very fact that Santo hired Harley, even temporarily, was a profound statement of his respect for Arlon.

The job at hand was a new county elementary school. Santo had subcontracted to build the concrete foundation. This entailed grading and leveling the site (which in return he "subbed out" to his brother-in-law, who owned the necessary heavy equipment), building the wooden forms, and after the drains and the water and gas lines were roughed in by the plumbers, pouring the concrete. In short, backbreaking manual labor. The seven-man crew worked from about 6:00 A.M. until sunset. When they were behind schedule, or if there was a bonus to be earned, they strung lights and worked on past dark. Most of the crew had nowhere to go anyway. Their wives and children were far away, and the harder they worked, the faster the time passed until it was time to go home.

Harley found himself in a similar if less permanent situation. The way he had it figured, a week's pay would make up for his losses at the courthouse and then some. By Sunday (the Mexican work week being six days, not five), he would be on his way west again, better off than he was before Arlon spotted him on the on-ramp.

Santo introduced Harley to the job foreman, Cruz Morales. After a short exchange in Spanish, which went by way too fast for Harley, the old man climbed back into his truck and headed off to open the beer joint.

Harley surveyed the construction site. The crew ranged in age from sixteen to about fifty. They paid little or no attention to the new man on the job. They were all far too busy. Granted, none of them had ever seen a gringo swing a mattock before. In fact, most had seen few gringos period. Their little village in hot, arid Chihuahua was not exactly a mecca for tourists, and here in Wheeler County their undocumented status forced them to keep to themselves. The little socializing that their Spartan existence allowed took place at Santo's place among themselves. It was simply none of their business who Don Santo chose to hire. Besides, in their world everyone had the right to work, to labor away the long dry stretches between the little pleasures in life.

Lunchtime. It always came as somewhat of a surprise when Cruz whistled loudly, forcing the air between two fingers pressed tightly against his lower teeth.

Cruz watched Harley unwrap one of Donna Ness's salami sandwiches while the rest of the crew made warm tacos from thermos bottles filled with *carne guisada* (beef tips in red chile gravy) and fresh homemade flour tortillas. He made a mental note to tell Harley that for three dollars a week, deducted from his paycheck, Don Santo's wife would make a little extra guisada and a few more tortillas each morning. Cruz was a firm believer in the necessity of a hot lunch for hard-working men. He spoke for the first time since work began early that morning.

"You speak Spanish?"

"Un poco."

Harley had picked up what Spanish he had during a six-
month stay in San Miguel de Allende, a town in the central
Mexico mountains long known as an artist colony and a refuge
for expatriate bohemians. He had followed a girlfriend there
shortly after being discharged from the army. When she ran off
to Mexico City with a Mexican actor, Harley hung around
playing Dylan and Beatles tunes in the gringo bars for a few
hundred pre-devaluation pesos a night. That is, until he became such a popular attraction with the rock-and-roll-starved
American community that the local musicians union com-
plained to Don Chucho Ybarra. Don Chucho owned all six of
the bars frequented by the writers, painters, and art students
who lived in San Miguel. The union's membership was largely
comprised of young, well-groomed *chicos* who made their living playing "Besame Mucho" and "Celito Lindo" for the tourists and squiring aging American and Canadian women to various social functions. They perceived Harley as a threat to their
livelihood. In reality, these musicians appealed to a totally separate audience. Nevertheless, the mariachis made their case to
Don Chucho, who unceremoniously showed them the door.
The union had no power in the little mountain town, and Don
Chucho was enjoying a marked increase in business since
Harley's debut. Three days later a group of five or six chicos
roughed Harley up a little on his way home from the gig.
Harley mentioned the attack to Don Chucho, and the next
day the president of the union local, a gifted young guitarist,
had both of his hands broken in several places. He never
played again. Harley caught the next train to the border, and
he never visited Mexico again.

"Vamanos, muchachos!"

Cruz was rousting the crew up from lunch, unknowingly
dragging Harley back through the years and across the border

to West Texas and the business at hand. He watched approvingly as Harley took his place alongside the others and set to work instantly, seamlessly becoming a part of the crew. Usually a new man needed time to get in the groove. Not this one. The other workers had never worked alongside Anglos before, so they didn't know what Cruz knew. Cruz was born in San Antonio and had built houses, apartment complexes, office buildings, and highways all over the Southwest and as far east as Chicago. Gringos didn't work like this. Even the most motivated Anglo worker lacked the fluidity, the poetry of motion Cruz saw and admired in his *muchachos* day in and day out. Cruz watched in wonder as Harley attacked the rock-hard Texas soil like a warrior, not a mercenary with his own agenda, but a soldier, an integral part of an army with a common cause — kill the day. Never simply let it pass but assault it, take hold of it, and wring the juices from it, drop by precious drop. You see, Harley Watts had been born with another gift in addition to his mastery of the highway. He also possessed an inborn ability to instantly home in on the essence of people, places, and things. It was simply not in his nature to take anyone or any experience for granted. Something reached out from deep inside of him. Touching. Tasting. Searching for the pulse. He didn't have it in him to just get by until payday, cash his check, and put Wheeler County behind him even if he tried. Harley felt what his fellow workers felt. He *knew* what they knew instinctively.

In time, Cruz Morales knew what Arlon Ness knew. They had both borne witness to something they themselves could only dream of. Something they admired, even envied, although they had no name for it. They were compelled to be near Harley, to soak up the very atmosphere around him for as

long as he graced their otherwise routine lives. Ironically, neither Cruz nor Arlon realized that as they lived vicariously
through Harley, he in turn depended on their stability. They
were now part of a vast network crisscrossing the country that
was Harley's lifeblood. Without Arlon and Cruz he couldn't
keep moving through their lives and on into the lives of other
solid citizens like them.

Payday came and went. Harley joined his coworkers at Santo's for a beer that first Saturday night. Arlon came in from the
second shift at eleven to find Cruz and Harley grinning from
behind a tabletop skyline of longneck beer bottles. The jukebox blared out equal doses of country and *norteño* music
fueled by a steady supply of red dye–marked "house" quarters,
courtesy of Don Santo. When closing time came, Harley and
Arlon stumbled to the car singing "Dim Lights, Thick Smoke,
and Loud, Loud, Music." Harley remarked at the novelty of
riding home drunk in the *front* seat of a police vehicle. Arlon,
caught up in the moment, suddenly yanked the big Ford over
on the gravel shoulder and locked up the brakes, throwing
Harley into the dash with a bump.

"You drive."

"What?"

"You drive. I'm gonna get in the back. No, really. I wanna
see what it's like."

Donna Ness was ripped from her sleep by a siren screaming in-
sistently, a few feet from her open bedroom window. She
threw on her old terry-cloth housecoat and ran to the door
with her heart in her throat, fully expecting to find Sheriff
Burke standing there bearing some horrible news about Arlon.
Instead, she was confronted with Harley Watts sitting behind

the wheel of Arlon's cruiser, siren blasting, blue lights flashing, grinning like a shit-eating dog. The only sign of Arlon was his boots protruding through the back passenger-side window as he collapsed in hysterics on the floorboard.

Donna wasn't amused. She hadn't seen Arlon this drunk since his first night home from the army. Oh, he'd stayed out late after softball games or at the sheriff's monthly poker party and come home a little lit, but ever since this Harley character showed up, he was somehow different. He whooped, hollered, and sang "Dim Lights" as she struggled to get him into bed. She cussed him out loud and warned of the dire consequences awaiting him and Harley if they woke the kids up. With all of the expertise of a good Texas girl with three brothers, she pulled off Arlon's boots and tucked him in with one leg hanging over the side, foot flat on the floor to stop the trailer from spinning.

Meanwhile, Harley had literally crawled in on his belly, remembering to keep his head low just like he had learned in Nam, until he reached the couch and passed out. Donna stormed out of the back loaded for bear, only to find him sound asleep, still fully clothed including his now concrete-covered boots.

"Well, shit."

It never ceased to amaze her how much grown men resembled her babies when they were asleep. Almost angelic. She shook her head and made that soft clucking noise with her tongue against the roof of her mouth that all women learn as soon as they are married. She pulled off Harley's boots and covered him with her grandmother's Texas Star quilt.

Any paycheck would have brought Harley back to even, but a series of events ensued, each delaying his departure another

week. Every payday began with Harley's best intentions and
ended with he and Arlon closing down Santo's beer joint.
At first it was simply a matter of math. Harley would cash
his check and begin buying rounds for his coworkers. Because he had no family and no responsibility, his income was
disposable; he never allowed anyone else to buy him so much
as a draft. At closing time, or more often the next morning,
a quick accounting invariably revealed a shortfall, and Harley's trip to the coast was put off for yet another week. Then
Cruz Morales, duly impressed with Harley's on-the-job perfor-
mance, offered him a raise, hoping to persuade him to complete the school job. Harley reluctantly agreed, and one Saturday gave way to another and weeks matured into months.

Arlon Ness, meanwhile, had appointed himself Harley's
outfitter and co-conspirator in this quest of his, this journey
into the wilderness that he himself could never make. He and
Harley, by now inseparable, spent their evenings at the beer
joint. Harley would sing and play his guitar, seasoning his repertoire with tales of the open road while Arlon made plans
for Harley's long trek west. Arlon would decide that Harley
needed a new sleeping bag or maybe one of those miniature
propane stoves. Cruz and Santo would kibitz and generally
concur. None of these amenities had ever been necessary before, but Harley always nodded and mumbled his agreement.
Months grew up to be years.

After a while Donna Ness gave up and began to join the
boys at the beer joint on Saturdays. That is, when her mother
or sister-in-law were available to baby-sit. She and Arlon would
dance to all the slow songs on Santo's jukebox, play pinball,
or shoot a game of pool. Over time she learned to like Harley, especially when after a few beers and some prodding from

Arlon and Cruz, he'd unpack his guitar. It seemed that Harley knew every song that could conceivably be performed on one old flat-top guitar. Dylan, Beatles, Haggard, Hank, and "Here's one by Woody by God Guthrie." There was always a steady flow of requests from the regulars at Santo's. After a few months Harley even learned some of Cruz and Santo's Spanish favorites, which were usually performed in the wee hours because Harley's Spanish seemed to improve drastically when he was drunk.

Donna privately observed that Harley had only to hold the guitar on his lap and he instantly became the center of attention. The songs themselves were merely interludes between the stories, the miles he'd traveled, the places he'd been, the people he'd seen. Donna and the others sat in rapt silence as Harley carried them with him to the far reaches of his range. New York, Boston, New Orleans, everywhere except Vietnam. Harley only included the miles he traveled under his own power in his musical travelogue. He viewed his entire tour of duty as an interruption in his normal life, as if some gargantuan unseen hand had scooped him up and deposited him in someone else's nightmare only to tire of the sport and drop him randomly back in his world to find his own way home. No one even knew Harley had been in the service except Arlon and Donna, and she knew better than to bring the subject up. She had lay in bed listening to Arlon crying softly in his sleep the first few years of their marriage. Then he simply stopped. Donna saw the same telltale trail of tears in the lines around Harley's eyes.

Maybe that was the beginning of the "thing" between her and Harley that everyone including Arlon sensed, but no one, least of all Harley or Donna, ever talked about. They all shrugged it off and lived for Saturday nights at Santo's. And

Harley played, and Cruz and Santo sang along out of tune, and Arlon and Donna danced. And they all drank.

Donna was always careful to stay just sober enough to drive home, or maybe she was afraid of that one beer that might nudge her over the line and into the arms of Harley Watts. After Arlon was safely tucked in, she'd sometimes sit on the edge of the couch and watch Harley sleep for a while. Then she'd suddenly shake her head to exorcise the demons and kiss him on the forehead the way mothers kiss children and retreat to the safety of the back bedroom.

For the first year and a half or so, the Saturday night ritual was religiously observed. The regimen dissolved so gradually that no one even noticed. Cruz left Santo's employ the winter after Harley hired on for a better job in Nashville, Tennessee. It seems a building boom in those parts had created a demand for skilled illegal labor and experienced bilingual supervisors. Harley accepted Don Santo's offer of the vacated position with characteristic reservation. Arlon was promoted to sergeant, which meant he was on call twenty-four hours a day. Harley maintained his residence on Arlon and Donna's couch for almost two years until one New Year's Eve when Arlon was called to the scene of a particularly nasty tractor-trailer accident on the interstate. He rushed off, blue lights flashing, leaving Harley and Donna alone and more than a little drunk. Nothing serious happened between them, but it was close. Too close for Harley. He moved out the next day and launched headlong into a stormy relationship with Delores Cantu, a fixture at the beer joint. He had spent the past couple of years politely refusing her advances, mainly because he had heard she was related to his employer. "I never shit where I eat," he informed Arlon. But Santo couldn't have been more pleased when Delores and Harley left the beer joint together for the first time.

Delores was Santo Guitierras's grandniece. She was what Arlon called "a handsome woman" — attractive, if a little hard looking, and a few years older than Harley. When she was seventeen, she had married a young man from Mexico who worked for Santo. She had come under the old man's patronage when her husband was killed, along with the rest of his crew, when their truck stalled on a railroad track up toward Wheeler. Delores was pregnant at the time. The trauma prompted a miscarriage and, because of the incompetency of the emergency room staff at the county hospital, a subsequent hysterectomy. When she recovered, she went to work behind the bar at Santo's. After work she had no one to go home to, so she didn't. She merely took five or six steps around the bar, planted her butt on a stool, and proceeded to get quietly shit-faced. All of these factors combined to make Delores a virtual white elephant as a marriage prospect. Santo figured he'd always have to take care of her until a faint glimmer of hope appeared in the form of Harley Watts.

Not that Delores and Harley rode off into the sunset and lived happily ever after. In fact, they rarely left the beer joint. Their frequent public fights became legendary. The thick smoky air in Santo's turned blue with shouted obscenities in two different languages. Beer bottles and ashtrays flew, always failing to find their mark, and observers were never able to determine whether to attribute this phenomenon to Harley's agility or Delores's lack of accuracy. This dance was performed over and over like some noncombative martial art, a kind of white trash tai chi. But the pair always kissed and made up before closing time, and Santo could only shake his head and deduct the damages from their wages.

Eventually the planning sessions for Harley's trip west stopped. The camping gear that Arlon had accumulated gathered dust in a closet in Santo's office. After a while Arlon and Donna stopped coming to Santo's altogether. Saturdays had become too busy as the kids reached Little League and Boy Scout age. Besides, as much as Arlon hated to admit it, it was becoming obvious that Harley wasn't going anywhere. He felt sometimes that Harley had let him down, although he would never have said that out loud. Harley was still his friend if no longer his hero.

In the winter of 1988 Don Santiago Guitierras died in his sleep of a massive heart attack. There was a bottle of antacid tablets by his bed. He evidently woke up believing he had heartburn, took a couple, and went back to sleep. Santo's younger brother, Victor, took over the construction business and the beer joint, but the sign out front still read "AAA" and everyone still called it Santo's. Harley was practically family by this time, so his job security was never in question. He and Delores still closed the joint every night, usually with an argument that could be heard in Las Cruces. The regulars had long since stopped asking Harley to sing and play or tell one of his road stories. Some of them weren't even old enough to drink when Harley first walked through the door with nothing but a backpack and the old guitar that now lay silent, entombed in its road-worn case under the bed at Delores's house. Harley was practically a local now and California was as far away as Vietnam.

Harley Watts looked down a long, flat stretch of I-40 west of Shamrock, Texas, hoping against hope that Arlon Ness would pull up alongside, just like he had ten years before to arrest him. But he knew better. The phone had awakened him just before 3:00 A.M. the Wednesday before. It was Donna. He still couldn't get over how calm she sounded. Arlon had made a routine traffic stop out on the interstate just before midnight. When he asked for the driver's license and registration, the stranger shot Arlon in the face three times.

Arlon died alone at the scene and was found hours later by a passing motorist. His killer was never caught. Harley spent the next few days helping with the funeral arrangements and taking care of the kids. Donna held up like a trooper right up until Sheriff Burke presented her with the flag that had covered Arlon's casket. Harley drove her home and held her as she sobbed for three solid hours. When she finally stopped, she suddenly kissed Harley hard on the mouth, unbuttoning his shirt as they slid to the floor. The kids were at her mother's, so they made love right there in the living room. When Donna finally drifted off to sleep, Harley slipped one of the throw pillows from the couch gently under her head, covered her with her grandmother's Texas Star quilt, and drove to Delores's. Being just as careful not to wake her, as he was Donna, he packed and walked out the front door leaving his truck in the driveway.

The big rig shuddered as it geared down and finally pulled over onto the shoulder about fifty yards beyond the spot where Harley stood.

"Well, I'll be damned."

He took off running, arriving at the cab out of breath and suddenly painfully aware of how out of shape he was. He hefted his guitar and backpack up into the cab, pushing them back into the sleeper as he settled into the shotgun seat.

"Where you headed, doll?" The feminine voice took Harley by surprise.

"California."

The handsome blonde behind the wheel laughed out loud as she set the beast in motion down the shoulder and eased it back over onto the highway.

"Well, this must be your lucky day."

JAGUAR DANCE

THE AMERICAN SAT alone on a rickety stool at a food stall in the central market eating a chile relleno with rice and beans, served all together in the same terra-cotta bowl. He spoke flawless Spanish with a central Mexico accent and his skin was tanned a deep dark brown, so only his height betrayed his ethnicity. Down here the mestizos average five feet five or five feet six at best, and the full-blooded Indians are even shorter. Closer to the border, some eleven hundred miles to the north, he might have even passed for a local, but not in Oaxaca.

The market was busy for this time of day. There was an intangible crackle in the air, and people were coming and going with a sense of urgency not normally encountered in the mountains of central Mexico. The old woman that ran his favorite stand told him that the old church across the plaza was celebrating its Santos — the feast of its patron, St. Anthony.

The American was instantly as excited as any school-age child in the plaza. He had spent enough years flying dope in and out of Mexico to know what was in store. First, there would be a procession. The parishioners would bear the effigy of the saint through the streets on their shoulders, the lovingly hand-carved and painted figure enshrined in glass and festooned with flowers. San Antonio was a large parish, so the fiesta would be grand and attended by people from all over the city. Street vendors would offer slices of watermelon and pineapple sprinkled with dried red chile and whole ears of corn roasted over charcoal in their husks. That night there would be great towers of fireworks (*el castillo*), showering sparks down on the young boys who risked not-so-minor burns to prove their bravery by running beneath them as they whirled and sputtered on the plaza before the old church.

The American loved Mexico. He had loved her for a long time now and he knew a lot about her. Beautiful things and ugly things, for when you love a person or a place long enough you learn her secrets, and if it's really love, you love her anyway. Hell, you love her more.

He knew, for instance, that in Mexico there had always been one law for the full-blooded descendants of Spanish settlers and another for mestizos, the progeny of their liaisons with indigenous peoples. There was, of course, no law at all for Indians. The authorities preferred not to deal with Indians, one way or the other. When they were included in the postcolonial culture at all, they filled the jobs no one else wanted — whatever work was dangerous, or low-paying, or both. They were soldiers (never officers — that was a privilege of class), policemen, and cowboys. The mestizos, subservient to the Spaniards and needing to feel better than someone, spoke of Indians in private as if they were animals, but face to face on the streets they gave them a wide berth, for privately they held them in awe. Indian women could be seen begging in the streets of any major city, but a mestizo who tried to make his living that way was arrested on sight. Outside of San Luis Potosí the Yaqui came, year after year, to gather peyote, the mythic hallucinogenic cactus. The American had seen them from the highway, fanning out across the chaparral, picking only the buttons that fell in their path. No one ever bothered them, even though possession of peyote is illegal. That was the Indian realm, and when a mestizo found himself confronted with it he crossed himself and went about his business. But let an Indian step into the mestizo's world, odds are he'll wind up face down in the street with the taste of tequila, blood, and bigotry in his mouth.

The American had been hanging around Oaxaca City for two weeks now. His plane, fueled up and loaded with a fortune in cocaine, sat grounded in a barn at the *rancho* of Don Emilio Esperanza just south of the city. He spent his days in the market and his nights in the cantinas waiting for word to come down from the mountains that the Federales had moved their portable radar to another pass. The Mexican government had received the new devices from the D.E.A. in the States, which hoped they would be used to curb the steady flow of narcotics across the border. Instead, the radar was used as a means to siphon money from the lucrative drug trade into the pockets of government officials. Time was, hundreds of low-flying aircraft slipped through the mountains undetected and unmolested every night. These days the *contrabandistas* had to wait on the ground for the all clear from their people inside the federal police. The waiting was always the hard part. The longer the wait, the more nervous the dope pilots became; they all knew that once in a while, when the heat was really on, a load was sacrificed. For appearance's sake, the erstwhile pilot would be betrayed by a telephone call, probably from his own supplier. It was getting so you couldn't trust anybody.

When the American started out in this business, back in the early seventies, the cargo of choice was marijuana and there was at least a modicum of honor among thieves. In those days most smugglers were simply hippie entrepreneurs with flight experience and a little more *cojones* than most. They chose colorful pseudonyms for themselves like Panama Red or Slippery Peso and spent their downtime in Manzanillo and Pelenque soaking up local color and indigenous mind-altering agents.

Then cocaine became fashionable back home, moving uptown from the shooting galleries to the discos, and things began to change. As pressure from the U.S. Coast Guard strangled the traditional marine routes through the Caribbean, the notorious Colombian cocaine cartels began looking for an alternate point of entry into the States. They were approached by their smaller-time Mexican counterparts with a proposal. Since the fifties the Mexican drug gangs had operated with relative impunity on their side of the border. They had cultivated the necessary channels through which to channel *la mordida*, literally "the bite" — the endless string of bribes expected by any public servant from the local police chief on up the line to Mexico City. The Mexicans even had an outlaw air force, tried and true, ready to deliver the goods to the North.

Coke was more compact, easier to conceal, and much, much more profitable. The American and his colleagues were suddenly catapulted into the big time. They bought expensive cowboy hats and boots, a lot of turquoise jewelry, installed eight-track tape players in their planes, and laundered their money through nightclubs in Austin or ski lodges in Jackson Hole. As the decade wound down, the smuggling business came to mirror its legitimate counterpart. Suddenly there was no room for romantics in the dope trade. The stoners and peaceniks had long since been left in the dust. This was the eighties and even in Latin America, Reaganoid pragmatism was the order of the day. The Mexicans, tired of settling for a middleman's stipend, eventually coveted the huge profits they funneled to the notorious Colombian cartels. They made their move — with a little help from the Spooks.

The American first heard about these new guys from other smugglers. They began popping up in San Miguel de Allende, Manzanillo, Key West, even Crested Butte and Jackson Hole. They stuck out in their polo shirts and khakis and their too neatly trimmed moustaches and beards. They looked like cops, and at first most of the pilots avoided them like the plague. The ice was only broken by the fact that some of the Spooks knew some of the pilots from Vietnam and other more obscure corners of Southeast Asia. Nearly every pilot left in the business, including the American, had learned to fly during the war, and some were no strangers to contraband when they came to Latin America. The Spooks said that there was a new deal, a real sweet opportunity for "guys like you." These days the real money was being made flying hardware (read: weapons) into and software (read: drugs) out of Central America for various contractors operating out of Panama and Costa Rica (read: the CIA).

The American heard tales in the bars and on the golf courses of fabulous fortunes being made. He did all right as well. There was no doubt in his mind that a lot of the cash generated by the goods he imported helped finance the "little wars" down south, but that was as far as he was willing to go. He had become somewhat of an anachronism: the only pilot in the business who stopped short of delivering weapons to CIA-backed guerrillas in Central America. He insisted on carrying only drugs or cash, allowing what was left of his conscience the luxury of plausible deniability.

*   *   *

The American finished his meal and lit a cigarette, pivoting on his stool to face the plaza in anticipation. He knew that when the procession reached the church, the Jaguar Dance would begin and he already had a ringside seat.

The Jaguar Dance was an echo of Mexico's pre-Columbian past. It had been practiced for a thousand years when the conquistadors arrived from gold-hungry Spain early in the sixteenth century. Finding no treasure in the mountains, the invaders moved on, leaving behind detachments of Franciscan friars to mine souls for the church. It had long been the missionaries' policy to allow their new flocks to retain some of their own rituals as long as they were willing to be baptized. The Jaguar Dance was one of many indigenous rituals assimilated into the church's calendar of feasts and celebrations. The Indians were just as pragmatic. The way they saw it, a people couldn't have too many gods in their corner, and furthermore, they saw no need to anger any spirit unnecessarily, even a strange, pale one from a faraway land.

Modern-day Jaguar Dancers were young Indians in their late teens and twenties. They wrapped themselves in jaguar skins, the head of the beast dried stiff to form a primitive helmet and the body draped about the shoulders like a cape. In pairs they faced each other, their slow circular movements emulating the big jungle cats, each sizing the other up. Suddenly they launched at each other, flailing away with clubs fashioned from stout sticks about three feet long, some with the actual paw of a jaguar fastened over the end. They struck each other again and again, each fierce blow announced by a resounding "crack" that echoed off of stone walls, like sharp peals of thunder in a box canyon. Sometimes the primitive headgear collapsed and the protagonists were severely injured. If you knew what to look for you could spot the veterans, for they wore their scars proudly. The American had even heard stories of dancers being killed. Although he'd never witnessed such a result, something primitive within him needed to believe that every word of these tales was true.

To the American the Jaguar Dance was the very essence of Mexico. Maybe it was simply that the Mexican government had outlawed it years ago and he had always seen himself as an outlaw. He had spent his life living in the margins while refusing to be marginalized. He saw something in the Jaguar Dance that few mestizos and almost no other gringo saw. He saw dignity. He knew that to an Indian, the Jaguar Dance was no mere nostalgic ritual but rather a form of cultural resistance, a public demonstration of one's "Indian-ness."

The mestizos didn't get it. Their European blood blinded them to the mysteries of Mexico. They had been so completely assimilated that the Jaguar Dance was something that "those *Indios* do to amuse the tourists." The tourists were even more clueless. They would climb to the top of the pyramids and look out over the lush canopy that concealed the foundations of a once magnificent city-state and see only undeveloped real estate. They equated the Day of the Dead with the Wal-Mart version of Halloween observed in the States, never following the processions to their destination in the local cemetery, where campesinos brought cakes baked in the shape of human skulls and picnicked with the spirits of their loved ones. They would witness the Jaguar Dance and see only quaint colloquialism and then return to their safe lives back up north with little or no understanding that they had witnessed magic. Real magic grounded in faith, heartbreak, and redemption.

Magic was important to the American. In all of his travels god knows he had witnessed enough of human suffering that a firm belief in miracles had become mandatory for his survival.

Magic was the grease that allowed humanity — a great ill-con-
ceived contraption, perpetually in a bind, and always at odds
with itself — to grind along age after age. His deepest dark-
est fear was that eventually there would be no Jaguar Dance
in Oaxaca and no peyote-gathering in San Luis Potosí. He
dreaded a world with no room, and no time, for *milagros*, or
pulque, or sugary skulls for the Day of the Dead. In his worst
nightmares new conquistadors came with their Holiday Inns
and satellite dishes and suffocated the mountains and blocked
out the sky. Then the grave robbers dug up every last remnant
of a once great nation's glorious past, tagged it and bagged it,
and auctioned it off to the highest bidder — and the ghosts of
Cortés and Coronado had their last laugh in Hell, raising their
glasses and drinking to manifest destiny.

The kid was ten years old, but he looked much younger to
gringo eyes. He ran all the way to the market from the home
of Don Emilio, his patron, a distance of nearly three miles.
When he finally managed to catch his breath and settle down
enough to talk, he delivered the message he'd been entrusted
with to the tall gringo with the scar under his eye.

"Don Emilio sends his regards and news from the mountains."

No further explanation was offered or needed. So much for
the Jaguar Dance. The American paid the old woman for the
meal, handing the change to the boy for his trouble as he hurried off to the taxi stand across the plaza.

As soon as the American dropped into "the slot," a long narrow
valley that served as the principal route for contraband from
Oaxaca through the Sierra Madre, he knew he was fucked.
The Bell HU-1 helicopter seemed to rise up out of the earth it-

self, rattling his hot-rodded Grumman Bearcat with the wash created by its massive main rotor. The Huey was of Vietnam vintage, the type the army used to outfit as gunships, and he knew them well. This beast, however, had been declawed before she was "presented" to the Mexican government. He'd seen lots of choppers of this type in Nam and he knew he could outfly it. His ride was faster and had more range. He nosed the plane up and blew over the top of the hovering Huey, leaving the startled Mexican pilot chattering impotently in Spanish over a high-powered public address system. Then the American simply put distance between him and the chopper until he reached the extent of its range, about two hundred miles.

The Huey was not the problem. In fact, the Federales didn't possess any aircraft that could catch him, and the Mexican Air Force's jets were never used to interdict drug traffic. Something was very wrong here. It was no accident that the chopper knew where and when to intercept him. He knew that there was probably a transponder hidden somewhere on the plane and that he would be tracked every inch of the way. He could outrun the chopper, and anything else they threw at him between here and the border, but there was no place on earth he could hide.

The American settled into a place where pilots go when the shit hits the fan — a surreal, focused space where everything seems to move in slow motion. He flew the plane by a kind of muscle memory, freeing his mind to run scenario after scenario.

What the fuck happened? Why me? Why now?

But he already knew the answers to those questions. If he closed his eyes he could almost see the dominoes fall, one at a time, each nudging its neighbor inevitably along in a sickeningly predictable chain reaction. Some politician in Washington or Mexico City promises publicly to do something about "these animals that are poisoning our children." Said politician needs a body count. Somebody's going down, but who? The selection process begins as soon as the Head Spooks in Washington send the word down the line through the Spook network that the Holy Covert Cash Cow is once again in peril. Loss of the drug trade means loss of funding for programs far too vital to national security to be entrusted to mere elected officials, much less the average citizen. That it appear to the world that a full-scale war on drugs is being waged is important. That the drugs, weapons, and money continue to flow is imperative. So a sacrifice to the Gods of Intelligence is prepared — and this time the American was the goat. It wasn't personal. It was simply his turn.

Fuck it. Just fly. They know you're here, so stay low, keep your eyes peeled and do what you do — fly. No running lights, no radar, just the Big Dipper on your one o'clock and the lights of Saltillo on your three. Yeah, this is real-live-outlaw-by-the-seat-of-the pants flyin', so just do what you do. Just fly.

Somewhere in the last low passes of the Sierra Madre east of Monterey the warning buzzer brought him nearer to earth and reality. He had burned far too much fuel evading the chopper and the Bearcat would never make the border. As soon as he hit the flat, seemingly endless desert of Coahuila, he started looking for a spot to set her down.

The Jaguar Dancer paced the plaza in semicircular arcs, back and forth, each ellipse slightly shorter than the one before, nearer and nearer the point in the center where his path would cross that of his counterpart on the other side. The other dancer was younger, faster, lighter on his feet, but there was something

*tentative about his approach. The older man, all of twenty-seven
and the father of six children, was somewhat of a local celebrity.
Beneath his jaguar robe he wore the scars of a few dozen such
encounters, mostly on his back and along his rib cage, but there
was a rather large strawberry-colored tattoo-like mark above his
left eyebrow, a souvenir of a close call some years back. When all
was said and done, he had kept his feet and finished the dance
and carried himself like his ancestors, a race of warrior-priests
who ruled these mountains for a thousand years.*

Sleeping bag. Canteen. Knife. Space blanket. Flare Gun. The
American limped around the floor of a deep ravine strewn
with the cargo of his shattered airplane and inventoried the
salvageable items he came across — *first-aid kit, camp stove.*
What began as a textbook dead-stick landing ended abruptly
in one of the ravines carved out of the desert by infrequent
but sometimes torrential rain. One minute the hapless craft
bumped and bounced across what appeared to be a relatively
smooth landing area. The next, its landing gear dropped into a
small chasm, shearing away and sending the Bearcat careening
at an odd angle on its belly in a cloud of dust. First there rose a
great rending of metal on rock and mesquite, cut short when
the now wingless airplane encountered a larger, deeper arroyo
and catapulted, end over end, scattering its cargo, along with
the personal effects of its pilot, like the contents of a broken
piñata. All the American had time to do was to fold his body
up like a lawn chair, jamming his head between his knees in
the classic duck-and-cover position he was taught as a child
growing up in the Cold War. All that he could think of as the
canopy shattered above (or actually, below his head, as the
plane was now inverted) was an old joke about the futility of
the uncomfortable maneuver in case of a nuclear attack. *How*

did it go? Place head firmly between knees. Kiss your ass good-
bye.

Somehow he had survived it all, with a few cuts and bruises
and a slightly pulled hamstring. He crawled out from under
the wreckage, dusted himself off, and immediately began gathering the gear he deemed essential to his survival. He located
a small backpack normally used to carry his "possibles" — a
nine-millimeter Ruger pistol with an extra magazine of ammunition, his shaving kit, a change of underwear, condoms, and
so on. All of these suddenly superfluous items, except the gun
and the spare clip, were left behind to make room for various
survival gadgets he was in the habit of collecting. His fellow pilots had always kidded him about this little quirk of his, calling
him Eagle Scout or Dudley DoRight. They preferred to deny
the possibility of going down or getting caught. They considered it bad luck to even talk about it. The American thought
about it all the time. It was as if he'd always known this day
would come, and now that it was here, he almost welcomed it.
He left the coke where it was. Whether he spent the rest of his
life in a Mexican prison or wound up somewhere in this desert
with a bullet in his head — even if he made it to the border
and managed to cross somehow — the American had made
his last run.

The Jaguar Dancers circled back and forth like a pair of pendu-
lums perfectly synchronized. Closer and closer they came with
each perfect concentric arch. The veteran moved slowly, surely,
never taking his eyes off of his partner, and there was a gravity to
his movements. Yes, "partner" would be the right word in Eng-
lish, even though they barely knew each other and were paired
off randomly, for the Jaguar Dance is not a competition. There
are no losers and winners per se. The only object is to deliver and

in return withstand blow after blow with a dignity that only In-
dians understand. But something was wrong. The upstart had
stopped in midcircle and suddenly lunged at the veteran, and as
he closed in, the veteran could smell both liquor and fear on his
breath, which came in short, desperate gasps. Before he could re-
act, the youngster swung his club, low to high in a terrible,
graceless, upper-cutting motion, smashing into the veteran's un-
protected chin with a sickening crack of wood against flesh and
bone. As the church and the stars and the shocked spectators va-
porized in a blinding white-hot flash of pain, the veteran cried
out, "No, no! You're spoiling it!"

The American was rescued from his nightmare by the sound of
his own voice. He had been screaming out loud in his sleep,
but now that he was awake he couldn't recall the words. He
didn't remember what he had dreamed, only that it was bad
and left a metallic taste in his mouth. He sat bolt upright and
spat several times, peering down at the thick spittle as it was
sucked down into the thirsty ground. He could have sworn he
tasted blood. He looked around him getting his bearings and
realizing slowly where he was.

He had walked for hours on a compass heading he had
calculated to intersect the nearest highway. When he finally
reached a shallow arroyo in sight of the highway, he dropped
to the ground where he was, wrapping himself in the space
blanket, the shiny silver side facing in to reflect and retain his
body's heat, and falling immediately off to sleep.

When the dream shook him awake it was just before dawn.
He raised himself up on his elbows and surveyed his surroundings. The highway was about fifty yards east of him. Back to the
west a series of vaguely connected arroyos stretched as far as
the eye could see. He retreated in that direction until he found

a depression deep enough to shelter him from passing eyes on the highway. He fashioned a lean-to from the poncho and ate a sumptuous feast of freeze-dried something or other from his cache of mail-order survival provisions. Pretty fucking disgusting. Then lying on his side and curling up into a fetal position to conform to the meager shade afforded by his makeshift shelter, he spent the morning poring over a military topographical map. By early afternoon he had a plan and he fell off to sleep again.

The American confirmed the highway was Mexico 57, a marginal two-lane blacktop by U.S. standards, but this was Mexico. By day 57 supported major truck traffic, banging and jarring along between Eagle Pass, Texas, and Saltillo. By night it belonged to contrabandistas and the Federales. The American would parallel the highway under the cloak of darkness, taking cover against the brutal Coahuila sun and resting during the day until he put a safe distance between him and what was left of his airplane. Then, somehow somewhere between Eagle Pass and Laredo, he would slip across the Rio Bravo del Norte (the Mexicans characterize the muddy, meandering stream Americans call the Rio Grande more accurately as "bold" rather than "large"). From that point on he would be hunted by one less government, but that was small consolation. It wasn't the authorities that worried him. It was those other guys, the ones that didn't see the lines on the maps. Men with no names, no family, no loyalties of any kind to encumber them on their mission. They were the real outlaws. Genuinely bad motherfuckers who could, and would, pursue him to the very ends of the earth.

For six cold, moonless nights punctuated by as many scorching, delirious days, the American kept moving. He could hear the traffic on the highway, and he used it to guide him; always staying out of sight but within earshot. When he came to a town he would fill his canteen, stalking the inevitable public faucet like a kid playing Capture the Flag at summer camp and then retreating into the harsh shadows cast by the lone streetlight. By the third night his supply of purification tablets was exhausted, and he had to resort to boiling water on a tiny propane stove he carried in his backpack. By the fourth day it became obvious that his survival rations weren't going to get him all the way to the border either. No matter how hungry he became, he had no designs on the scrawny chickens he occasionally encountered on his water raids. Water was one thing, but the average campesino kept poultry for the dark brown free-range eggs they laid. Only rich people could afford to slaughter them for meat. Besides, water doesn't make much noise when you steal it.

By sunrise of the seventh day the American found himself on the outskirts of a town — a good-sized town, much larger than the hamlets he had encountered so far. After consulting his map he determined that he had reached the town of More-los, one of twin villages (the other was called Allende) that straddled 57 on the west and east, respectively. That meant that less than thirty miles to the northeast lay Piedras Negras and the U.S. border.

OK. He'd fall back to the nearest cover, make camp, and get some rest. He'd apply bandages to blisters and shed excess weight — camp stove, propane bottles, poncho — in fact, all he really needed now was the compass, the pistol, and a little water. When the sun went down he'd cross the highway and head north. When he reached the river he'd simply parallel the border, just as he had the highway, keeping sufficient distance to avoid the authorities on either side. Then somewhere in the empty expanse between Piedras Negras and Nuevo Laredo he would wade across the river to Texas.

The Jaguar Dancer opened his eyes and then closed them against the brightest light he'd ever seen. So bright in fact that his eyelids no longer afforded him a dark place to hide, and he perceived a tall figure in silhouette behind a screen of brilliant orange shot through with an intricate latticework of his own tiny blood vessels. Somehow he knew that the Watcher would wait patiently until the dancer's eyes adjusted to the light and then answer all of his questions.

"Spirit, why did the young one want to harm me?"

As soon as the words left his mouth, he was immediately ashamed, for himself and his people, for the names of the spirits were long since forgotten. The Watcher smiled and answered both questions.

"The young ones are becoming like those who enslaved them. They believe only what they can see with their eyes. Our names are not important. You gave us the names, after your own language and customs. We have no need of names here."

"And where is here?"

"The place from which we have always watched over you."

"Am I to stay here with you, then?"

"No, there is another place for you. You are here to have your questions answered, then you will move on."

"And the young one?"

The Watcher's very presence darkened.

"He has many trials ahead and this place is lost to him. He will have to find his own way. You will see him where you are going but not for a long, long time, I fear."

Something told the Jaguar Dancer that his audience was at an end. Still, his worldly curiosity begged another question.
"*Spirit, are there . . . ?*"
But the Watcher was gone.

The American jumped up out of a dead sleep. There was someone standing, no, crouching over him. He rolled to his left, grabbing the pistol from its hiding place beneath his backpack/pillow and thumbing the safety off as he sprang to his feet. The intruder immediately dropped to the ground, involuntarily assuming a submissive posture, his arms covering his head.
"No tirotear!"
Don't shoot. The small dark figure writhed on the ground and frantically issued an unbroken stream of Spanish that went by at a clip too fast for the American to comprehend. This was no *Norteño*; the accent was all wrong. He probably wasn't even Mexican. As the American's eyes adjusted to the moonlight, it became apparent that the man looking up at him in terror through almond-shaped, coal-black eyes was definitely Indian and probably Mayan.

His name was Eligio and he had traveled from the mountains of Guatemala to this spot within a stone's throw of the U.S. border in a little over three months. He had left his home with nothing. His village had been leveled by the Guatemalan army in a crackdown on leftist guerrillas believed to be operating in the area. Many innocent people were killed, including his wife and four children. Eligio had survived only because he was one of the guerrillas the army was looking for, and he had been training a few miles away when they entered the village. He and his comrades had watched helplessly from the next ridge as their village burned until they were fired on by a government patrol. In the confusion he had become separated from his unit and made his way down into Guatemala City, hoping to lose himself in the largest city he had ever seen. After hiding for a while with members of the movement there, it was determined that Eligio had been identified and that Guatemala was no longer safe for him. In fact, his presence had become a danger to the movement itself, as the government was determined to find him. He would have to go. He crossed the Mexican border late one night, in the trunk of a car driven by a sympathetic Irish priest.

Since then Eligio had learned there were larger, more frightening places than Guatemala City. He had seen Oaxaca City, Puebla, and Cuernavaca. He had even spent a month in the largest city in the world, although he had no way of knowing that at the time. He never got as far as the broad boulevards and great stone monuments in the city center. To Eligio, Mexico City was the vast, fetid, refuse heap on the outskirts of town where the remnants of Mexico's native peoples picked a wretched living from the garbage cast off by the mestizos. They were Coras, Huicholes, Otomis, Nahuas, Mazhuas, Tascos, and a hundred other once great nations, although many no longer remembered the names of their own people. Here they were just Indians.

It was uncomfortably close to the descriptions of Hell that the nuns at the mission school had used to scare the children of his village into applying themselves to their catechisms.

Eligio decided that he would try to make it to the United States. It couldn't be any worse than Mexico, and he had a cousin who was working in a garment factory in California somewhere. Maybe he could find work and start over. Maybe the revolution was over for him.

A series of stolen rides on freight trains and third-class buses had brought him to Piedras Negras on the Texas border, but it didn't take long to discover that the last few miles of his journey would be the most difficult. The word was that there was something strange happening over on the American side. All along the border, from Texas to California, the border patrol was out in force. Officers normally engaged in drug interdiction had been reassigned to high-density patrol operations along the routes favored by illegal aliens attempting to enter the country. Even the border patrolmen themselves didn't know what all the fuss was about, although there were rumors that a major drug kingpin, a gringo with a scar on his face, was expected to attempt to cross the border sometime in the next few days. The general consensus among the thousands who, like Eligio, waited along the border for an opportunity to cross over to a better life was that, at least for now, there was only one safe way to go. He would need to contract the services of a *coyote.*

Coyote is the border term for a smuggler of human beings. Originally they were simply guides who knew the best routes across the shallow river and the habits of the authorities on both sides. They would lead small groups of "illegals" on foot in a single line, retreating to their own side of the river once their charges had crossed. Lately the most successful coyotes had developed a more modern, efficient technique. They used medium-size box-back trucks, cramming in as many as fifty human beings into the dark, airless cargo bays for a bone-jarring ride over rough unpaved roads. Communicating with accomplices on the other side by means of cellular phone, the driver would make a mad dash through the inevitable holes in the border patrol's dragnet, traveling cross-country if necessary until they reached a safe place to unload. From there his clients were on their own. Some made it past the interior check-points, some didn't. The coyote didn't care one way or the other. He already had their life's savings in his pocket and another load booked for the following night.

Eligio asked around and was directed to an upholstery shop at the end of an unpaved, dead-end street. The skinny coyote with the large gap between his front teeth quoted sums too huge for Eligio to fathom. Back in his village in Guatemala no one ever learned to count higher than ten, and the very concept of addition and subtraction was totally unknown. If a person went to the market to buy eggs, he purchased them one at a time. Twenty centavos for one egg. Then another twenty for another and so on, until he or she had what looked like enough eggs. The coyote talked so fast, Eligio was lucky to glean a word or two. He spoke a bizarre brand of border Spanish heavily laced with American street slang, and he talked with his hands as well, opening and closing them again and again to display all ten of his fingers — once, twice, after three times it wasn't necessary that he continue. Despair descended on Eligio like a fast-moving cold front. *No one has that much money,* he thought. He would never cross the border, and it was only a matter of time now before he was caught. He would be deported home to Guatemala and quickly executed, probably without so much as a hearing. Just a ride out into the jungle and a pistol shot to the back of the head.

But no one in Mexico was looking for Eligio. As long as he didn't try to return home to Guatemala, there was no immediate threat to his life. He was only in danger of living out his life on the streets of one border town or another, scuffling for scraps with the other Indians.

For lack of any clear course of action he wandered around

the city keeping to himself, until hunger forced his hand. He stole an apple from a fruit stand in the market. The proprietor spotted him and called for the police. Eligio fled, managing to lose his pursuer after a few blocks and then hid under a railroad bridge and ate the apple, ravenously like a scared animal looking around after every bite for any sign of danger. As soon as it was dark he struck out across the desert, walking all night, afraid to get near the roads for fear he would be arrested. The apple was meager fuel an for all-night hike over rough terrain, and he was getting weak and on the verge of tears when he spotted what appeared to be a corpse lying face down in an arroyo. He overcame his horror enough to inch in for a better look. Perhaps the poor soul had some money. Before he could find out, though, the body sprang to life and he was looking down the barrel of the American's pistol.

In his first conversation with a human being in almost two weeks, the American picked up two vital pieces of intelligence: that this Indian was no threat to him, he was only hungry, and that he wasn't the only poor sonofabitch wandering around this desert looking for a hole in the border. The American had attempted to cross for three nights in a row only to be turned back by unusually dense patrols on the Mexican side. He had finally given up and decided to get a little sleep, hoping against hope that things would look better in the morning, but in reality he had begun to lose hope.

Alliances are, more often than not, forged in the fires of desperation. But actually, Eligio and the American had a lot in common. They were both outsiders in their present environment, isolated by ethnicity on the surface and politics at the core. That the two of them should find each other in an arroyo in the middle of the night was instantly recognizable to both men as magic, plain and simple. A ray of hope piercing the gathering darkness just as they were both ready to give up. Separately they were at the end of their respective ropes. Each lacked a resource that the other possessed. The American had money to pay the coyote to take them across the border. Eligio knew where to find him and could do so without attracting undue attention.

It was decided that they would sleep in shifts, the odds being decidedly against another kindred spirit wandering around the chaparral. The American took the first watch, as Eligio was exhausted. The American could hear the Indian's stomach growl from across the arroyo and it reminded him there was one last freeze-dried meal in his backpack. He had become so sick of them that he had gone without food for two days rather than face another of the tasteless concoctions. He showed Eligio how to prepare it with water from the canteen. Eligio inhaled the mess and the American shook his head and laughed.

"Man, you were hungry."

Eligio didn't understand. He thought it was possibly the best meal he had ever had. He was even more impressed when he learned that it was the last, and he was humbled by his new companion's generosity. He wrapped himself in the space blanket, rolled over, and was almost instantly asleep.

The plan went like this: At first light Eligio would go to town and speak to the coyote. As long as he stayed clear of the market, his stolen apple was not likely to become an issue. He would make the deal for both him and the American, telling the coyote that his brother would accompany him on the crossing. Eligio would pay the customary 50 percent deposit to reserve their places on the truck. It never occurred to the

American that with the entire price of a crossing for one in hand, Eligio could simply leave him there in the desert, and it never occurred to Eligio not to return as promised. They both knew that trust is a powerful form of magic. It requires that the practitioner believe in forces he or she cannot see. Practiced faithfully it could bring lives, even worlds together.

The coyote saw Eligio coming from the top of the street. He remembered him from a few days before. "What does this *pinche Indio* want?" he wondered out loud to the other coyotes hanging around the shop. "He has no money. He told me as much himself."

The coyote saw this kind all the time. They came from El Salvador, Guatemala, and the state of Chiapas in southern Mexico. Ignorant, backward people with no idea what it takes to make a living up here in the North. They were like children, handing him cigar boxes and tobacco tins stuffed with crumpled small-denomination notes.

"Is this enough?"

"No, no, I told you! The price is one thousand pesos per person!"

They would confer among themselves and produce a little more money they had hidden away somewhere and add it to the offering.

"And this?"

"No, no, no! One thousand pesos! One thousand!"

They were impossible. *And these pendejos want to go to the States? They won't last five minutes in L.A. or Chicago or even San Antonio! They are only Indians! No matter. Let them go. They would learn, and the coyote would stay right here in Mexico and get rich.*

Eligio approached the upholstery shop with his hat in his

hand. "Buenos días, Don Flaco." Indians always address mesti-zos as "Don" or "Doña" if they expect a response.

"What do you want? I told you, the price is one thousand pe-sos. Five hundred now and five hundred when we leave. Now go away and come back when . . ."

Eligio checked back over his shoulder and then produced ten one-hundred-peso notes, one at a time from the sweatband of his hat, laying them in a loose stack inside the crown. The coyote looked both ways and then scooped the notes up and counted them.

"Two o'clock tomorrow morning. Behind the *petróleo* station."

Around midnight they started for town.

The American wore an old blanket draped around his shoulders, serape fashion, and Eligio's straw cowboy hat pulled down low over his eyes. He looked like an extra in a bad spa-ghetti western. They had contrived the costume to make the American's height less obvious. By slouching and bending his knees a little with the blanket wrapped around him and being careful not to stand right next to Eligio, they managed to make their way through the deserted streets without an incident. They found the coyote and his cohorts behind the *petróleo* sta-tion as promised.

"This is your brother?" the coyote asked Eligio.

Eligio's heart stopped. "Yes, Don Flaco, my brother, Mi-guel."

The coyote looked up at the American and then back down at Eligio. "What happened to you?"

He laughed a great belly laugh that seemed out of place from one so slight of frame. His *compañeros* laughed. Even the American, unable to restrain himself, laughed as well. The only one left out of the joke was Eligio, the Indian.

The coyote was just as suddenly all business. "Where is the rest of the money, hombre? Ahh, bueno. Get in the truck. You will both be Americans by sunrise!"

For an hour and a half after the doors were shut, the American sat on the floor in the front of the old decommissioned U-Haul truck with his back wedged into the corner and his knees drawn tightly up against his chest beneath the old blanket. It didn't take long for it to get hot, but by then it was too late to remove his makeshift disguise, as there was simply no room to maneuver. He and Eligio were the very first passengers to board the vehicle, but now there were at least thirty, maybe even forty other souls crammed into the nearly dark, nearly airless space. They were mostly young men, but there were several women as well, some with small children. The children were amazingly quiet. They had traveled a long way mostly by night from places far to the south, and they had learned to be silent and nearly invisible. They were already outlaws at a tender age.

In total darkness they waited for the engine to start. To the American time seemed to crawl along at an excruciating pace, measured by the pounding of his heart and the throbbing in his legs. To the Indians (including Eligio) time divided into increments smaller than a season was meaningless. Their ancestors had been great astronomers and makers of elaborate calendars. When the Spaniards came they abandoned chronology altogether, the way that prison inmates do, because for people in bondage the very passing of time is torture.

The American could still see the last image that his brain recorded before the doors were closed. Faces — some young, some old. They hung there in the darkness, ghostly negatives in iridescent silver-green. After a while they began to fade, to shift and dissolve one into another like spent smoke rings — and then they disappeared altogether, as the truck's engine hacked and sputtered to life.

Almost immediately the truck's human cargo began to take a beating. The American felt every cut and bruise of the plane crash out in the desert all over again. He estimated their speed at at least forty miles an hour, and he tried to envision the terrain they traversed — down rutted washed-out roads, then cross-country, rattling down the length of deep arroyos, and then airborne for an instant as they emerged on the other end. One particularly hard bump prompted him to call out loud, a grunt really, barely audible as it escaped through clenched teeth. In the darkness the singularly human sound was heard by everyone in the truck over the engine's roar and the gnashing of worn-out gears against a maladjusted clutch. Now the others knew that he wasn't one of them. An Indian never cries out. No matter what. No amount of insult or injury could ever be dignified with an acknowledgment of pain. To an Indian the only dignity that remains is to accept any indignity in stoic silence.

But now it didn't matter. They were all merely payload now. Once the door was pulled down and padlocked shut, they were all on more or less equal terms. The American finally had his first real taste of what it was to be an Indian.

When the truck finally lurched to a stop, it was sitting on a slight incline so that the weight of all of the passengers standing in the back of the truck shifted toward the front and bore down on the American and Eligio. He heard the wheels spin and the gears grind and the clutch slip — they were stuck! Then the engine died and he heard the driver's and passenger's doors open followed by footsteps fading quickly away in opposite directions — and then nothing. Absolute silence be-

yond the confines of the abandoned truck. The only sound inside was that of its occupants breathing, and even that was so
soft that it was nearly inaudible. Without understanding the
need to conserve oxygen and limit the carbon dioxide produced by their breathing, these people seemed to know instinctively when it was best to minimize their impact on their
environment, when to become invisible and still, to live only a
little. The American attempted to get up, but Eligio's hand on
his shoulder gently but firmly held him in check. The message
was clear. Wait.

He tried his best to wait like an Indian. He settled into the
darkness around him until he found a place where the heat
didn't matter and where his heartbeat didn't try to keep time
with a clock somewhere in England that he'd never seen. His
breathing became a slow, shallow sip in through his nose and
out through his mouth. After a while he began to get the hang
of it. It was kind of like flying. Just let go and do it. He didn't
notice when the sun peeped through a tiny hole in the sheet
metal above his head and focused a slender, pale, yellow beam
on the brim of his hat. He wasn't aware that as the hours passed
the temperature inside the truck reached upward of 130 degrees, and that what little moisture was harbored in the hard,
lean, malnourished bodies of its unconscious occupants now
hovered above them in a collective cloud of invisible vapor,
waiting to be sucked out into the desert air along with their
spirits the instant the door was opened. If it was ever opened.
Getting to his feet was out of the question. There was simply
no room to move. Once in a while, he would lose the groove
and he wanted to scream at the top of his lungs, but that impulse always died somewhere between the spark in his brain
and the note in his throat. There was no use. No one would
hear him and it would be a waste of precious moisture and en-

ergy. So he settled back even further into this new sanctuary he'd found within himself. This Indian place. He was now part of something older than the pyramids in Tulum and Pelenque. Older even than the Jaguar Dance. A tradition of magic and mystery that bound a people together and allowed them to not participate in their own extinction, to move on to the next world as a People, unbowed and unconquered. They slipped away into unconsciousness one by one, not like refugees, but like wizened warriors returning home to live and fight another day. The American followed them — part of the way.

When the Spooks came across the old truck, they almost just left it where it was. It was sitting at the bottom of a fairly deep arroyo buried up to its axles in sand and gravel.

"This must be the runner the immigration guys were chasing," one of them said. "They said they lost it when it doubled back across the border. I guess they were wrong."

When they popped the hasp open with a tire iron and pulled open one side of the double doors, the smell was overpowering.

"Jesus Christ, wetbacks."

Some had died on their feet and when the door was opened they collapsed and fell backward into the arms of the Spooks, who let them fall to the ground, wiping the smell of death from their hands on the front of their fatigues in disgust. They didn't even bother to try to determine how many bodies there were in the truck. If they had they would have counted thirty-one adults and six children. They just wanted to get as far away from this rolling mausoleum as possible. They would call Immigration when they got back to town. They left the truck just like they found it — except that now the door was open.

They were in such a hurry, in fact, that they never knew that the breath of freshly oxygenated night air that flooded the truck found its way through a tangle of just-starting-to-decay flesh to revive its one living occupant. Another hour and the American would have been dead as well. He survived only because he was better nourished and his body's greater mass simply retained more moisture for a longer period of time. He had given himself over to dying, without a sound, without a futile struggle to defile the moment of death.

He came back from the brink slowly. There was a kind of sadness in finding that he was still alive and that his traveling companions including Eligio had gone on ahead without him, a sense of profound loss that he would carry around for the rest of his life. He had learned enough in his short time with the Indians that he knew to lie still until it was dark and the truck's interior had cooled off a little before wriggling his way up and over the bodies and out into the cool night air. He sat on the ground for a while until the strength returned to his legs and then hauled himself to his feet, took a compass reading, and struck out due north, carefully avoiding the roads until he was well past the checkpoints.

The Jaguar Dancer's path was paved with an intricate mosaic of multicolored marble-size cobblestones. They appeared perfectly round and they were smooth and comforting against his bare feet. There was jungle on both sides of the path rising to a height sufficient to block out any appreciable amount of sunlight, but the path seemed to generate its own illumination. There were birds of every color and size, including some truly fantastic varieties the Jaguar Dancer had never seen before. The jungle was lush and green and the trees were heavy with bananas, mangoes, and papayas, and monkeys played games of chase in the canopy above. The Jaguar Dancer heard a low coughing sound behind him and he knew that when he turned around the jaguar would be there waiting for him. Together they followed the path until the jungle opened up into a beautiful valley ringed by majestic mountains. Maize grew in long even rows nourished by perpetual sunlight and cool clear clean water from a mighty river that knew no dry season. There were great temples and houses of stone decorated with a skill and artistry the likes of which the Jaguar Dancer had never seen before. The people held their heads high, and they spoke and sang of the old songs in strong clear voices. Not only were all the Maya there but so were all of the other peoples, and they called the names of their nations out loud as they greeted each other. Some had been enemies for a thousand years or more, but they would dwell together in this new place in peace under the care of the Watchers until the plague from across the water had run its course and the world was once again a safe place for magic.

TANEYTOWN

It's springtime up in our holler. I been fishin' down to the creek already. It'd be warm enough to go swimmin' 'fore long. When I was lil', I'd just shuck out my overhauls an' jump in nekid. Mama say I'm too big for that now. Say I'm a man now, an' a man cain't go runnin' 'round nekid like no wild Injun. I tol' her I didn't feel like no man, an' she say if I'm big enough to smoke and drink, I'm too big to go runnin' 'round with my tallywacker hangin' out. Say if I don't keep my drawers on down to the creek from now on Jesus would get me.

Mama tol' me whatever I do don't never go to Taneytown. Say they don't like niggers down there. Me an' Mama an' my little brother, James, the only niggers up in our holler. Everybody else up in here white an' they like niggers just fine. I use to go fishin' an' swimmin' with the Mangrum boys some. Tommy Mangrum, the one that's 'bout my age, use to say how niggers is good luck an' how I'm double lucky on account of I'm a little slow. When folks say how I'm slow that don't mean runnin' or nothin'. James say I'm about the fastest thing in this holler when it comes to runnin' an' swimmin', such stuff as that. They just mean I'm a little slow in the head. James say I'm a retard but if anybody else call me that, he'll whup they ass. That's on account of he's my brother.

Some folks in our holler goes to Taneytown all the time.
James go two, maybe three times a week with a load of firewood. He bring me 'backer an' papers to make my cigarettes
an' stick candy an' tol' me all about things down there. He tol'
me 'bout them other niggers live down there, but they all
bunch together down by the swamp an' keep to they selves.
Say in the summertime the skeeters get so big they carry them
niggers' babies off in the middle of the night. I'm glad I don't
live by no swamp.

Last summer Mama went off to Gettysburg. That's a big
place, bigger than Taneytown an' Mama say they's a big battle
there a long time ago between the good white folks an' the bad
white folks an' the good white folks whupped the bad ones, so
Abraham Lincoln come an' made a great speech an' set all the
niggers free. She went off down there with a white man name
of Luther. I ain't never seen him before but he all right, I
guess. He rode me an' Mama down to Simpson's store in his
big, fine automobile an' bought me a root beer an' a pack of
Luckys. Mama say her an' Luther was goin' to Gettysburg to
get some money. Say they be gone all night an' James'd watch
out for me.

Soon as Mama's gone James an' the Mangrum boys took
drunk. They give me some whiskey once but it make me sick
so they say they ain't wastin' no more on me. I don't want none
no how, on account of it always make 'em act a fool. First they
laugh an' cut up a lot, an' that part's all right, on account
of they kinda funny, but after that they always fuss an' fight
somethin' awful. One time James bit a chunk out of Harvey
Mangrum on account of him drinkin' all the whiskey up.
Then they jus' pass out.

This time I climb up in the loft until James an' them Mangrums is asleep. I can always tell on account of James snore somethin' awful. I tips out the door, bein' extra careful not to let it slam.

It's a fine night out, nice an' warm, an' the crickets an' the tree frogs must think so too on account of they jus' singin' they hearts out. The moon's big an' bright an' mean lookin', an' I could see every rock in the county road the way it go windin' down the holler all white an' shiny like the belly of a great long snake. I just keep on goin'. Sometimes I want Mama or James to holler at me to stop, but they never do so I just keep on goin' an' goin' on past the creek, on past Simpson's store 'til I come to where the county road meet the blacktop highway.

Never in my life did I come so far down the county road. Never past Simpson's. Never past the creek, on my own. I just stand there for the longest time, on that bright, shiny white gravel, the toes of my shoes almos' touchin' the blacktop.

That blacktop highway is the blackest thing I ever did see. Blacker than ol' man Maury's dog. Blacker than my brother James. It look to me like a well full of dark, cold water so deep that the moonlight sink straight to the bottom an' never come back up an' so cold it'd take my breath if I fall in an' I'm sucked down an' drowned, an' never heard of, ever again.

But I ain't sucked down an' when I hunker down an' touch that blacktop it's warm an' it's hard as river rock, so I takes me a step. Then I takes me another'n an' another'n an' 'fore too long I'm walkin' down that ol' scary blacktop highway all by myself.

There ain't no other soul stirrin' out, an' all I can hear is my own two feet on the blacktop, an' my own heart thumpin' in my own chest, an' the crickets, an' the tree frogs an' God only knows how far I walk an' then . . . I stop an' look up, and the sign say "WELCOME TO TANEYTOWN, MARYLAND."

I reckon I walk all night long, 'cause the sun is peekin' over the ridge 'bout the time I gets to Taneytown. They got some big fine houses down in Taneytown, with the greenest grass I ever did see out front an' all kinda flowers an' such. Seems like the longer I walk, the bigger an' finer them houses get. Never in all my life did I see so many people. They's all kinda people. They's tall people an' short people an' old people an' lil' chidren an' mostly they white, but a few of 'em niggers like me. An' everybody busy runnin' here and there an' in a great hurry an' if anybody pay me any mind at all, I cain't tell. Some just bump right into me, like to knock me down in the street an' just keep on goin', like I ain't even there. Make me feel teeny, tiny, an' kinda lonesome an' I start missin' Mama an' James a lil' bit, but I just keep on goin'. I seen things I ain't never seen before. Things James tol' me 'bout, but I didn't hardly b'lieve him, like the bobber shop an' the dry goods store an' the five an' dime. I never knew they was so many things folks could buy, an' it's all shiny an' new. I don' b'lieve they's never been nothin' bran' new in our whole holler.

On down the street a piece, they's a whole mess of folks standin' in line at this one big place with a great, bright sign, all lit up on top. I don' know what the sign say on account of I cain't read but I b'lieve that's the picture show. My brother James tol' me all 'bout it. I would sure love to see *that*, all that cowboys an' Injuns an' cops an' robbers an' such, but James tol' me it cost two bits an' I ain't even got a nickel. But James seen it once, with his firewood money. He say he gonna carry me sometime, but Mama say, no.

"Don't never go to Taneytown."

Then she whup the tar outta James.

I jus' walk aroun' that big ol' town gee-gawkin' for the longest time. My neck's sore from lookin' up at the big fine

houses. Next thing I knows, I'm tired an' I just cain't walk no
more. I come to a big, white church, but I don't dare go in
there, on account of I'm scared Jesus'll get me for runnin' off
like that. Mama say he always watchin' me. I'm so tired on account of all that walkin' I just drop down in the churchyard
with my back up next to an ol' oak tree. I reckon I jus' fall off to
sleep, directly.

When I wake up it's evenin' time already, an' I reckon I slept
under that ol' tree half the day. I'm as hungry as an ol' bear an'
I start thinkin' maybe I better get myself back home where at
least I know they's some cornbread left over from dinner yesterday, if James ain't eat it all. I take off walkin' back through
Taneytown, back the way I come. Directly I come on a big
empty field, in between two big houses.

They some boys there, an' they playin' baseball. I like baseball. I play baseball all the time, back in the holler, with James
an' the Mangrum boys, before they jus' up an' quit one day.
Mama say they outgrowed baseball. Say they got they mind on
girls now. I tol' Mama 'bout big ol' Molly Tipton down the holler can smack a baseball a mile and catch pretty good too an'
she a girl. Mama say it ain't the same thing.

I watch them Taneytown boys play ball for the longest time
an' they all pretty fair ballplayers, but they cain't none of 'em
run like me. I guess they don' see me standin' there they
playin' so hard. I don't make much noise. Mama taught me
that when the social worker come up the holler when I was lil',
an' I'd hide in the cupboard 'til she gone. Mama say if I make a
peep the ol' witch'll find me an' take me away an' I won't never
see James or her ever again. Social worker don't come aroun'
no more. I guess she just give up.

Directly, one of them boys pop up a fly ball, way up in the
air. It fly up so high, like it ain't never, ever gonna come back

down. When it finally do, this poor ol' boy in the outfield lose it in the sun an' that ball bounce right off the top of his head an' knock him silly. Everybody run to see if he all right an' then they all stop . . . an' turn aroun' . . . an' they all look at me.

I'm laughin' my ass off. I don't even know I'm laughin' 'til all them Taneytown boys turn aroun' an' stare an' then they jus' drop they mitts an' they all comin' at me, all at once, even the boy that was hit by that fly ball, so I reckon he ain't hurt too bad. They start into hootin' an' hollerin' an' they all still comin' right at me an' I'm scared, an' I'm glued to that spot. Cain't run, cain't talk, cain't even spit. Next thing I know, they all jus' standin' there in a ring all aroun' me. Then one of 'em, a great big ol' boy, what was the pitcher, say "What you laughin' at, nigger?"

I been called a nigger all my life, by all them Mangrums an' ol' man Simpson, an' jus' 'bout everybody else up in the holler, even James, an' he a nigger too. It don't bother me none. But the way them Taneytown boys say it, it sound . . . different. Sound nasty or somethin'. It make me feel real bad. Kinda sickly an' scared inside. Now they all hollerin' 'bout nigger this an' nigger that an' I'm powerful scared. Scared enough, I reckon, to unglue my feet an' I take off runnin'. Them Taneytown boys take off right behin' me, an' they chunkin' rocks and dirt clods an' such, but I jus' keep on runnin', back through the middle of Taneytown. I'm runnin' as fast as I can but they so many folks out an' about, carryin' sacks and bundles an' such, I cain't get me no runnin' room. Them Taneytown boys cain't run like me, but they jus' knock over anybody get in their way, ol' women, lil' children, it don't matter to them, they jus' keep on comin', an' they still hollerin', an' I'm still runnin' an' then . . . I'm flyin'. Tumblin' through the air, ass over teakettle an' landin' hard on my face in the blacktop street.

I roll over an' look up at the biggest man ever I saw. He got great, long, black side whiskers an' a big ugly nose, looks like it been broke two, three times. I know who *he* is 'fore he ever open his mouth. Sheriff John Law. James tol' me all about him.

Ol' John Law, he seen me come tearin' down through the middle of his town an' jus' sticks his big ol' foot out an' trips me. Them Taneytown boys see me go flyin' an' they all just stop in they tracks.

"You, boys! What's goin' on here?" The big pitcher boy speak up an' tells the sheriff they jus' "chasin' this nigger back down to the swamp." I don' have to hear no more. I jump up an' run like a spotted ass ape, 'fore that sheriff can grab me, an' I'm gone through the front door of the dry goods store an' out through the back. I don' want me no part of no swamp.

Them folks in the dry goods store, scream an' holler somethin' terrible when I come flyin' through there, knockin' over stuff an' slam that back door with a great bang. They probably don't see nothin' but a whoosh, I'm movin' so fast. An' then I'm outside in that alley an' I jus' keep on runnin' even though I don' know where I'm goin', an' my legs jus' a'burnin' an' my heart jus' a'thumpin' like it's gonna jump right up out my mouth. I come to a railroad track but my breath give out an' I cain't run no more so I jus' stop. I turn aroun' an' look an' there ain't nobody back there, so I look aroun' an' find me the sun, so I know which way to go. My brother James learned me that.

So I'm walkin' down the railroad track now, an' I'm huffin' an' puffin', tryin' to catch my breath. I'm stickin' to that railroad track, on account of I reckon I won' meet nobody that way, but I'm wrong. They's a great, long, tall trestle that stretch 'cross the riverbed, an' when I'm smack in the middle, I look up ahead an' there stan' that big ol' Taneytown pitcher, along with another boy, waitin' on the other side. I turn to run an' I get 'bout two steps an' stop. They's two more Taneytown boys comin' at me from that end. I reckon I'll jump an' swim for it, on account of James always say I swim like a fish, but the trestle too high an' the river ain't but a foot or two deep right there. I look back toward Taneytown. Here them boys come. I look on down the way I was headed an' here come them other two. I ain't never been in no fight. I don' like fightin'. James always whup up on anybody bother me anyway. I don' know which way to go an' I'm scared to death. All of a sudden like, that big boy come runnin' an' he jump on me like a dog an' knock me down in that rough ol' railroad bed, an' sit on my chest an' it hurts an' I cain't breathe an' he starts hittin' me in the face an' callin' me a dirty nigger an' I'm even more scared but then I get me a hand free an' I reach down in the leg pocket of my overhauls an' find . . . my big ol' Randall knife that James give me.

I never hear such a terrible sound in all my life as that knife make when I stick it in that poor boy's back. It made a kinda sick, crunchy noise an' then there was a hiss like a tire goin' flat. That ol' Taneytown boy jus' flop down on top of me an' I scream like a girl an' push him off an' jump up an' he just stare up at me an' make a bubblin' sound when he try to talk. Then he don' make no sound at all, but he still starin' right at me. I look aroun' an' them other boys already gone, runnin' like scalded dogs back across the trestle to Taneytown.

I look down at my knife an' that poor boy's blood all over it. I drop it an' run like I never run in all my life, 'cross the trestle an' down the railroad track. Pretty soon, I come up on the blacktop road an' I turn right, an' I jus' keep on runnin', jumpin' in the bushes an' hidin' everytime I think I hear somethin' comin'. They ain't nothin' movin' on the highway, I reckon 'cause it's Sunday, an' everybody in church, but I keep hearin' footsteps behind me an' I'm scared so I cut 'cross somebody's cornfield an' them cornstalks rattle an' make a terrible racket. I hit the woods on the other side an' I'm still runnin' to beat the Devil his self, briars an' brambles grabbin' at me, tearin' up my overhauls. All of a sudden like, I run up on a creek, *my creek*. Now I know which way to go. I run along the bank of that creek, my good ol' creek. I don't even slow down when I come to the county road. I jus' turn left an' keep on runnin' an' I don't stop 'til I'm back home an' in my bed. I'm so tired I fall right off to sleep.

Mama come home that evenin', jus' 'fore suppertime. She say I look like hell. I don' say nothin'. James don' say nothin' neither, on account of he know Mama'd whup his black ass if she foun' out he took drunk an' lost track of me. Mama jus' let it go.

A little while later, me an' James an' Mama was down to Simpson's store. We had to walk on account of Luther don' come aroun' in his big automobile no more. Ol' man Simpson say he jus' been down to Taneytown an' everybody down there jus' a buzzin' 'bout this crazy nigger from down to the swamp. Say he murdered a white boy, from a good family, not that trash down by the river, up on the train trestle. Say the boy was stabbed in the back. The other boys with him say it was a nigger that done it an' that they couldn't do a thing 'cause he was at least seven foot tall an' besides he had him a gun an' a Randall knife. The folks down in Taneytown went plumb crazy an' they fetched torches an' lanterns an' bird guns an' such an' they all go down by the swamp an' commence to roustin' niggers out they beds, hollerin' about burnin' down niggertown if somebody don' give the murderer up. They was draggin' niggers out in the street an goin' through they pockets lookin' for that Randall knife an' that pistol an' shore nuff one of 'em had him a Randall knife stuck down in the top of his boot. It even had a little blood on it. That poor ol' nigger cry like a baby an' beg an' carry on about how he foun' that knife on the riverbank, underneath the railroad trestle. They don't pay him no mind. They jus' tie him up an' haul him off an' string him up from the trestle. Ol' man Simpson say he hung up there for a week.

Wintertime come an' the wind whistle down the holler an' through the cracks in the wall next to my bed. Some nights it put me in mind of that hissin' sound that Taneytown boy made an' I cain't sleep. When I do sleep I still have them dreams, now an' again. Sometimes I dream 'bout that Taneytown boy. Sometimes I dream 'bout that poor ol' nigger swingin' from the trestle. Either way, they both always starin' right at me through them froze eyes. I wake up screamin' like a banshee an' wake half the holler up. I jus' tell Mama I was dreamin' 'bout the social worker.

I ain't never goin' down to Taneytown no more.

BILLY THE KID

THIS TOWN has gone to hell. I'm not talkin' about all that shit they built downtown along lower Broadway like the Hard Rock, Planet Hollywood, and the NASCAR Café. That kind of stuff's all right, I guess. I mean, if you're into that kind of thing. Those places mainly attract tourists, and tourists spend money, and that means jobs, and God knows we needed them around here. I'm talkin' about the heart of Nashville. I'm talkin' about Music Row. If you don't believe me, just take a walk down Sixteenth Avenue, or Music Square East as they call it nowadays, and tell me what you see. A lot of ugly-ass brick and glass monstrosities. Everyday they tear down another one of those beautiful, old, converted Victorian homes that until recently housed recording studios, music publishers, and booking agents. Oh, RCA, Columbia, and some of the other major record labels were ugly enough, but they were all in a bunch down at the bottom of the Row, and what do you expect from a bunch of Yankee carpetbaggers anyway? In the old days no one in the homegrown music business here felt a need to put on airs like that. They just plugged along in their little makeshift, shag-carpeted offices — that is, if they had an office at all. There were a lot of hip-pocket entrepreneurs on the Row who did business in the bars. Some of them were full of shit but now and again one would hit a little lick and make out like a bandit and buy the drinks for a while. Then country music got big. I mean really big — too big for its britches, if you ask me, and now every time you turn around they're knockin' down another landmark to make room for god-knows-what until I don't even recognize this place anymore.

When I first came to Nashville in 1960 things were different. Don't get me wrong. There were just as many assholes in the music business then as there are now, and there was always a lot of bad music. Some things never change. Like this beer joint, here. Only the name has changed. When I bought it from Old Man Cantrell, back in 1962, it wasn't called the Idle Hour. It was the Blue Room then, but it looked pretty much the same as it does now. Same jukebox, shuffleboard machine, and pool table. Same stale beer smell knocking you down when you walked through the door. . . . You'll get used to it.

The faces have changed some too. Some are dead. Some got out of the business. Some never got in the business, just gave up and went back to wherever they came from — Mississippi, Alabama, Georgia, Kentucky. There were plenty from up North as well. Don't think they don't have hillbillies in Pennsylvania, West Virginia, and Maryland. They even got them in places that don't have any hills to speak of like Michigan. They all got off the bus downtown full of piss and vinegar, and sooner or later they'd all find that ugly blue door, over there. Most wouldn't stick. They'd hang out a few months at best until they ran out of money or doors to knock on and then they'd be back downtown at the Greyhound station with a long face and a longer ride home. Most wouldn't even say goodbye; they'd just sort of fade away. If they were any good they usually faded in as well, easing their way into the scene as word got around about their songs.

Not Billy Batson. He hit that door like a freak winter tornado, letting in a lot more sunlight than the regulars were accustomed to in one dose. I remember exactly what I said to J. W., my bartender.

"Oh, shit. Another Texan."

But I was wrong. Oh, Bill was from Texas, all right. He had the hat, the attitude, and the penchant for communicating in analogies. If you asked him, or any other Texan for that matter, a simple question his answer usually began with "It's like . . . , " and then you might as well make yourself comfortable. The town was overrun with them in 1974. Willie Nelson had pulled up stakes and moved home to Texas a couple years back and was now having the last laugh on all the yahoos on Music Row who said he couldn't sing. Meanwhile back up here in Tennessee, we were ass deep in cowboy hats.

But Billy had a seriousness about him, a kind of built-in immediacy in his every move. He didn't wait for his eyes to adjust to the dim light in the bar. Instead the light adjusted to him as he cut a path straight to the bar, swung his lean frame up onto a vacant stool, and ordered a draft. Without a second's hesitation I drew this perfect stranger a beer and started a tab on my little pad beside the cash register. Not knowing his name at the time, I wrote "The Kid" above the first of many little pencil marks, each one representing Bill's good intentions and my small contribution to the Real Thing. I knew, even then. We all knew, every last hillbilly in the bar. Even Faron Young and Porter Waggoner stopped shooting pool and bitchin' about not being able to get played on the radio anymore when Billy walked in.

Everyone liked Billy. There was something about him that made you want to root for him. He was rail-thin but he didn't appear frail. He had bottomless brown eyes framed in a shock of jet-black hair, which he anchored in place with an even blacker cowboy hat. When he smiled, and he smiled a lot, he lit up the whole room — even the Blue Room. Women wanted to take him home and feed him (at least). Men wanted to be him, but they never let their envy go to rancor. I've been around songwriters all my life and I can tell you, they can be a jealous bunch. I stood behind this bar many a night and listened to them bitch when one of their compadres got lucky and an established recording artist recorded his song. Then when the man of the hour arrived a little later, butter wouldn't melt in their mouths. They knew the lucky writer would be spending money that he hadn't made yet (and might never make, showbiz being what it is), and they weren't about to let pettiness get in the way of a free beer. Somehow Billy was exempt from all that. We all just knew, somehow, that he was something special and we treated him accordingly, even before we ever heard him sing a solitary song.

And what songs. He must have had a hundred. I hired Billy to play Wednesday, Thursday, and Friday night, down here at the joint. I paid him twenty bucks a night but I put an old plastic bucket out for tips, so he did all right. Billy couldn't have been more than twenty, and he looked like he could have been even younger, but when he sang you *believed* that he had been a foot soldier at the Battle of Shiloh or a train robber or a rodeo clown. He had songs that could transport you down to Mexico or across the Rocky Mountains or deep into the Louisiana bayou country. He played guitar hunched over in a straight-back chair like an aging Delta bluesman, caressing and massaging the instrument until the rhythm oozed out like sap from a sweetgum tree. None of us had ever seen anything like it. Not even the old-timers like Vernon Agee, who was sitting in Wesley Rose's office the day Hank Williams walked in off the street, fresh from Alabama. The way Vernon tells it, anybody with one eye and half sense could tell that ol' Hank wasn't long for this world. You could smell death on him from a hundred yards away. But Billy was all about life and all of its contradictions. He was young but wise, weathered but innocent, possessed of a tough hide and a tender heart.

The first time Annie Winters saw Billy she stopped and stood in the doorway over there, hypnotized until he finished the song he was singing, creating a small traffic jam in the process. When she finally made her way across the room to the bar, she headed straight for me, ignoring J. W., who like everyone else in town was more than a little sweet on her.

"Who is that?"

"Nobody, just the best damn songwriter that ever walked into this bar."

"No, you old goat, I mean what's his name?"

Well, that was that. Every heart in the Blue Room broke simultaneously that night, or at least all those of the masculine persuasion. Bill never had a chance. No sooner had he finished his first set when Annie intercepted him before he could even make it to the men's room.

Annie was a twenty-two-year-old student nurse over at Baptist Hospital. She grew up in the white trash quarter of West Nashville knowing that if she didn't do something different from her friends and older sisters, the best she could hope for was a trailer out on River Road and a husband that didn't hit her. Nursing school seemed like her best shot, although if you ask me, she would have made a fine doctor. She was smart as a whip and drop-dead beautiful. She wandered in here one afternoon during midterm exams looking for a quiet place to study and have a beer in peace. There was no one around but J. W. and me, and we got to talking about music and books and Nashville, and before long it was closin' time. A couple nights later Annie was back, and it wasn't long before she was a regular. She got to know the writers and became the object of nearly every hillbilly in town's obsession, the "Sweetheart of the Blue Room" you might say. But when J. W. made last call she always went home alone.

That is, until Billy hit town. That first night they spent Billy's breaks huddled in the back booth. Within a week you never saw one without the other, and even J. W. had to admit that they made a handsome couple. They were young and in love, and it was a truly beautiful thing to witness. It was a Music Row fairy tale and we were all supporting characters.

Well, this ain't that big a town and word got around fast that there was a new kid up from Texas who could write 'em, play 'em, and sing 'em. Billy hadn't been around more than a month when the sharks started circling. Normally this town doesn't go out of its way to support singers who write their own material because they upset the balance of nature. Nashville is the last Tin Pan Alley, a place where writers who don't perform can come and trade half their copyrights for a steady paycheck and a shot at a six-figure payday down the road if they're lucky. Lately the record labels have come into their own, but this town was built by music publishers who cut deals over strong drinks and hundred-dollar-a-hole golf. The most successful publishers were the ones that never forgot that without the writers they were nothing, all the while managing to never let on to the writers themselves. Not being shy about cutting the right producer or label executive in on the action also helped a lot. Once in a while one of the singers got smart and got in the publishing business, but for the most part they were too busy out on the road to figure out that while they were away from the farm, the fox was in the henhouse. "Artists," as they are known in showbiz vernacular, were and are expendable.

But Billy was the exception. The Kid was a breath of fresh air in an oxygen-poor environment, and even the slimiest reptile to crawl out from under a desk on Music Row instinctively knew better than to profane the moment. Billy had a habit of looking you right in the eye when he talked to you, as well as when he listened, and the local lizards found that unnerving as hell. The only one in the bunch who could take the heat was Mason Bell.

Mason Bell was one of the Young Turks in the music business. The son of a wealthy real estate developer from Meridian, Mississippi, he had earned a law degree from Vanderbilt University. The venerable institution's campus backed up to Music Row, and sometime during his second year Mason caught the bug. His family was, naturally, horrified when he announced his plans to open a publishing company but young Mason was determined. Beginning with thirty thousand dollars his father grudgingly released from his trust fund, he opened a small office over on Nineteenth Avenue and signed a couple of writers. Within a few years the new company developed a reputation for nurturing talented young songwriters who worked outside of the usual Nashville musical formulas. Mason never discouraged his writers from coloring outside the lines, so to speak, and the result was that Mutiny Music, as the company was called, began to get attention from outside of Nashville. Rock bands in L.A. and New York wrote their own material, so the publishing business on both coasts began to concentrate on signing recording artists with major-label record deals. Songwriters began deserting the coasts like rats from sinking ships and settling in Nashville. If, say, a film company needed material for a project, they had to look to their country cousins. Mason Bell was in on the ground floor of the soundtrack business in Nashville and he never looked back. By the time Billy walked into the Blue Room that afternoon in 1974, Mason had money to spend and a hunger to find something new, something that Nashville and the world had never seen or heard before. Billy fit the bill to a T.

Billy and Mason hit it off instantly. They were an odd pair with absolutely nothing in common on the surface, but Billy trusted Mason and Mason, for his part, never violated that trust. Mason signed Billy to a copublishing agreement, asking for only 10 percent of the income from his songs in return for administration rights, an arrangement unheard of before (and since) in Nashville. He functioned as Billy's personal manager as well, never asking for or receiving any additional compensation. When the record labels on the Row started snooping around, Billy told them to talk to Mason, who in turn politely passed. No "Vice President in Charge of Cows and Pigs," as Mason privately called them, was going to sign Billy. He would negotiate with their bosses in L.A. and New York only. The odd thing was that even at the height of the hoopla there were almost no hard feelings. Even the publishers and labels eliminated in the first go-round remained supportive of Billy and offered to do whatever they could to help the project along. By this time those of us who had been around for a while were starting to get suspicious. Something was going on here. Something you don't run across everyday.

Meanwhile, rather than wait on the lawyers, Mason decided to put his own money up for studio time so that Billy could begin work on an album. That way, he figured, the record could be completed in a more creative atmosphere without interference from carpetbaggers. Mason called Ronnie Rector, the veteran recording engineer and producer. Ronnie had started out in Memphis in the early sixties and had recorded a wallful of platinum albums in his career. When he heard the kid sing for the first time, he canceled six months of bookings in his studio to clear the decks for an album project on an unknown, unsigned singer-songwriter from Texas everyone in Nashville was calling Billy the Kid.

As work began on Bill's record, a routine quickly developed. Billy, Annie, and Mason would show up here at the bar about noon with a cassette tape of the previous night's work and a dozen Krispy Kreme doughnuts, and I'd put on a pot of coffee. Then we, the few fortunate few, would listen in wonder as Billy's songs, some of which we had known since their conception, emerged like newly morphed butterflies from the raggedy-ass speakers behind the bar. I mean, we knew the kid was good, but this record had a weight, an undeniable gravity to it. J. W. said it was like going to church. I wouldn't know, but it did have a lot to do with faith.

Bill's music reminded me why I came to Nashville in the first place. I had a suitcase full of lyrics, just like everybody else. What I needed was a bucket to carry a tune in. No musical talent whatsoever. Once I got to know some real songwriters, I learned quickly how hard it is to marry words and music into a seamless creation. Even then, it isn't really a song until you sing it. It doesn't have to be pretty, but it must be heartfelt. When a writer first breathes life into his latest creation, that instant — when an idea borne on a melody leaves his lips — is rare and magical. Most people never get to witness that. Even if they do, they might not get it. I didn't. Not at first anyway, but once I did I quietly quit writing and settled into shoes I could fill. That happens. Sometimes our lives don't turn out the way we plan. I guess that's why J. W. and me get along so well.

See, J. W. is my hero. He didn't set out to be a bartender. In fact, J. W. Allen was the most heavily recruited football player in the state his senior year at Nashville/Overton High School. He went on to the University of Tennessee in Knoxville with a full ride and was a shoo-in first-round draft pick until his left knee exploded trying to haul in a short pass against Alabama in Tuscaloosa. Lying there in the hospital after his surgery, he knew from the look on the doctor's face and the fact that the coach hadn't bothered to come visit that his football days were over. He resolved right then and there that he wasn't going to feel sorry for himself. He'd had a good run and he came home with his head high. I admired that in J. W., so when I had to face the fact that I would never be a world-class songwriter I took his lead. I became instead a kind of patron — part coach, part banker, with a little psychiatrist thrown in. Every writer that could really write came to me for advice or a small loan or an ear to bend. The greatest part was that I got to hear the best new songs in Nashville before anyone else.

See, in those days the songwriters were the bohemians in Nashville. They were hillbillies all right, but they were hillbillies with vision. They moved fast but they saw the world around them in a kind of slow motion. On a good night they could stop the world dead in its tracks, dissect an otherwise ordinary moment, and glean the beauty and the drama hidden there in plain view. The best writers routinely cranked out three-and-a-half-minute jewels that owed as much to Tennessee Williams as to Hank. Some of them had even read William Faulkner and Ernest Hemingway. Those that didn't read (because of lack of education or exposure or both) learned their craft from the born storytellers they knew back home in Bumfuck, Wherever. Stories about coal mines and moonshine and movin' it on down the line. They carried layer upon layer of memories along, in their hearts, to Music City U.S.A. Of course, their eyes and ears were always open for anything new

— raw material that they could add to their stockpile. Sometimes, when the stars lined up and the beer-to-marijuana ratio was just right, one of those tales would just bubble up to the surface, and before it had a chance to hit the ground, a *real* writer would impale that moment on a No. 2 pencil and mount it on a yellow legal pad. God, I wish I could do that.

And we all wished we could do it like Billy. But we couldn't, and we knew it, so we settled for the next best thing. We witnessed. We watched and we listened and we wished Billy and Annie well, almost selflessly. I say "almost" because there wasn't a hillbilly in the Blue Room who didn't harbor a secret hope in their heart of hearts that somehow they could absorb some of that something that burned so brightly in Billy by osmosis, if they could only stand close enough to the flame.

In a little over a week Billy and a hand-picked band of musicians had recorded fourteen basic tracks. From where we were sitting, Billy Batson had just recorded the greatest collection of songs ever produced in Nashville. There wasn't an ugly puppy in the litter. But Billy wasn't satisfied. Listening to the best of his short life's work coming back at him through the speakers, Billy heard something we missed. In between the tracks, amid the tape hiss and electronic hum, he heard the rest of his record. The stuff that he carried deep inside of him and needed to say now that he had the chance.

Seven of those original tracks were chosen for the record, and while Mason and Ronnie applied the finishing touches, Billy hunkered down in the studio lounge and commenced to write again. Any writer in Nashville would have given his or her right hand to write any one of the seven songs that were discarded. Nevertheless, they were cut off the reels and relegated to the tape vault. By the end of the second week, with Billy running in and out of the control room to approve overdubs and final mixes, the original seven tracks were completed. Then one morning at the Blue Room, while Mason, Ronnie, J. W., and Annie sat with their mouths hanging open, Billy got out his guitar and unveiled six new songs.

Mason immediately got on the phone and started rounding up the band. With all of the principals assembled at the studio by six that evening, work began anew. The process was a little different this go-round. Instead of cutting one basic track after another, leaving added instruments and background vocals for later, Billy decided that he wanted to complete each track, overdubs mixing and all, before moving on to the next song. That gave most of the band the day off once a suitable "basic" was recorded — but nobody went anywhere. Everyone hung out until the wee hours of the morning just to see how the fruits of their labor turned out. After all, they had an emotional investment in this project. About eleven o'clock on Friday night of the third week, Ronnie sequenced the completed album and we all squeezed into the tiny control room to listen.

Each new song fit into a specific gap in the previously existing material like a lovingly handcrafted component. Now the best record ever recorded in Nashville was damn near perfect. There were plenty of rough edges but no flaws. One song segued seamlessly into the next, and every time you thought you'd heard what surely had to be the best track on the record, the next would come along and rattle you to your very core. We laughed. We cried. J. W. threw up. Excitable boy, J. W.

When it was over, we sat there for what seemed like an eternity. It wasn't one of those long, uncomfortable silences but rather a delicious, dreamlike state, each of us in our own little world that Billy had created, savoring the last chord as it faded away like the afterglow of a Caribbean sunset. It was Mason who came to first.

"Ronnie, let's hear that again."

Most of us stayed and listened once more to the whole damn thing. Mason, J. W., and I hung around while Ronnie played it back a third time, and Annie and Billy slept on the couch in the back of the control room. We finally stumbled out of the studio a little after six, squinting against the first rays of a new day — hell, a new era! Just as we were getting ready to pile into Mason's Cadillac and head to the Waffle House for breakfast, Billy spoke for the first time all night.

"Guys, Annie and me are gettin' married."

It was perfect. We made plans over steak and eggs and about a gallon and a half of coffee. The kids were in a hurry, so the date was set for the following Friday. I suggested that the ceremony take place at the little wedding chapel over on Eighteenth but Annie was adamant. She had first laid eyes on Billy in the Blue Room and by god she was going to marry him there. J. W. borrowed an aging Cadillac stretch limo from his brother-in-law, who owned a funeral home over in East Nashville, and his sister made the cake. Annie made her own dress; it was simple and white and beautiful beyond words. Her daddy passed away when she was ten, and I was honored when she asked me to give her away. Mason and Ronnie were in charge of cleaning Billy up. They hauled him out to the mall and tried on a half-dozen suits, but not one hung right on Billy's angular frame. His was a body built for jeans, so they settled on brand-new black jeans, a matching denim jacket, a white tab-collar tuxedo shirt, and a string tie. Oh, and a new hat and new boots, black of course.

Mason contributed his family's beach house in Gulf Shores, Alabama, for the honeymoon. When the vows were all said and the songs were all sung, the cake was cut and the bouquet was caught (by J. W.; once a wide receiver, always a wide receiver), Billy and Annie ducked into the limo in a shower of rice and rode around the corner to the Hall of Fame Motor Inn. There, Annie's truck waited gassed up and decorated with the usual streamers and lewd best wishes scrawled in tempera paint. Mason slipped Billy an envelope containing a couple hundred bucks and his Exxon card for gas. We all watched the happy couple drive off into the night as proud as any parents. We couldn't have Annie, or write like Billy, but we could tell our children that we were there, witnesses to Hillbilly Camelot in all of its fleeting glory.

With the newlyweds off to the beach, we all slept in on Saturday morning. I didn't even bother to open the beer joint that night. J. W. hung a hand-lettered sign on the door that read "Closed in Honor of Mr. and Mrs. Billy Batson." On Sunday we opened at noon as usual so the Texas contingent wouldn't miss the Cowboys game on TV. After the game the regulars sat around and listened to a cassette copy of Billy's record over and over until closing time.

By noon on Monday, Mason Bell's phone was ringing off the hook. The head of every record label in New York and L.A. had received a tape copy of Billy's record the week before and every last one had submitted a bid. By close of business on Wednesday, Mason had narrowed the field down to two serious contenders. He booked a seat on the 9 A.M. flight to L.A. and walked down to the joint to tell J. W. and me the news. Mason had two nearly identical offers on the table. Both included big cash advances, bigger than any new artist in Nashville had ever dreamed of. There would be more than enough money to defray Mason's costs and make a down payment on a new house for Billy and Annie. There would even be enough left over for the couple to live on for the next year, if they were careful. Even more important than the money was the structure of the deals themselves. Under both agreements Billy would maintain ownership of his master recordings and lease them to the label for ten years. At that time Billy could renegotiate his royalty rate or take his catalog elsewhere, an unprecedented arrangement for an artist of any stature. I bought a round for the house and proposed a toast to Mason's negotiating genius. Mason shook his head.

"I wasn't me. All I did was drop the tape in the FedEx box. They want Billy that bad. Hell, they're just like us. They just want to be associated with the Real Thing."

"All right then," I conceded, raising my mug up for everyone in the joint to see.

"To the Real Thing!"

What followed was a succession of rounds, purchased for the most part on credit. J. W., keeping track of the tabs, had developed a world-class case of writer's cramp by about nine. We drank to Billy and Annie. We drank to Ronnie's ear. We drank to J. W.'s impending marriage; after all, he had caught the bouquet. By midnight everyone was hammered and the evening still stands today as the least profitable twenty-four-hour period in the Blue Room's unprofitable history.

About 1:30 Mason, realizing that he had an early flight, pried himself off his stool and lurched for the door. Before he could get there, the phone rang. J. W. answered it.

"Hey, Mason, it's for you, dude."

Maybe it was more good news. No one had ever called Mason at the joint before. A hush fell over the room as Mason crossed back to the bar and reached for the phone. Maybe it was another record label, doubling the existing offers, and they simply couldn't wait until morning so they tracked Mason down at the beer joint and we would all be witnesses!

"Yeah? What? No, wait a minute — how do you know? What kind of an accident? — no — no — I'll be right there."

Mason handed the phone back to J. W. and plopped on a barstool. Before he said a word we already knew something was terribly wrong.

Billy was booked to play the Blue Room on Friday, as usual. Gulf Shores is a day's drive and he wanted to get back to run through some of the new material with the band, so they decided to head home early. He and Annie had started out Thursday morning for Nashville. They made it as far as Culman, Alabama, just south of the Tennessee line. There, a southbound tractor-trailer crossed the median and hit Annie's little truck head-on. The Alabama state trooper who called Mason said that "according to the accident report," the driver of the big rig simply fell asleep and Billy and Annie were killed instantly.

I wonder how they know all that? That the truck driver fell asleep. Does "instantly" mean that it didn't hurt? I hope so. Did Billy and Annie see that truck coming in time to know what was going to happen and to say "I love you"? God I hope so. How the hell would the Alabama State Police know what causes the world to suddenly spin out of control for an instant, changing everything forever. The trooper said that they found Mason's Exxon card on Billy's body, they contacted the oil company and took it from there.

Everybody who was anybody in the music business attended the funeral. The little chapel out at Inglewood Cemetery was bursting at the seams. The regulars from the beer joint came of course, all of the best songwriters in Nashville and some of the worst. There were also folks there I only knew by name or reputation, who had never set foot in the Blue Room or heard

Billy sing. They only knew that something was going on and that this might be their last chance to get close to it. I overheard a conversation between two perfect strangers who both swore that they knew Bill back in Texas. One said that he and the Kid were traveling partners and that they'd hitchhiked up to Tennessee together. The other claimed to have given him his first guitar lesson. I don't believe that I realized then that I was witnessing the birth of a legend at my friend's funeral.

When it was all over, we laid those poor kids to rest side by side with a single simple marble headstone inscribed:

BILLY AND ANNIE BATSON
BORN
FEBRUARY 15, 1955, AND APRIL 6, 1952
STOLEN FROM US
MAY 11, 1974
THE BEST OF US ALL

That night back at the beer joint there was a small private gathering. In attendance were J. W. Allen, Ronnie Rector, Mason Bell, and myself. Mason said that his answering machine had run out of tape after twenty-seven messages, mostly from record labels, but now that Billy was gone, film companies wanting to buy his story were coming out of the woodwork as well. Not to be outdone by the Alabama State Police, some of the more resourceful executives tracked down the number at the Blue Room. The phone rang constantly and we did our best to ignore it until, finally, J. W. ripped it off the wall, prompting a small standing ovation. Then we got down to the business at hand.

The discussion was short and sweet. As it turned out, we were all of the same mind anyway. Every label in the business wanted Billy's record. Every screenwriter, hack biographer, and talk show host wanted a piece of the action as well. It was easy to see that there were literally millions of dollars to be made, mostly by Mason, but if Billy's record was released and was a hit (a certainty, it was simply too good to miss), we could all sell our stories about Billy to the highest bidders. Talk shows. Tabloids. More money than any of us had ever seen or would see in our lives. Billy had no family at all and Annie's would only piss it away. With Billy not around to keep everyone honest by his very presence, there would be nothing to stop the feeding frenzy. We all agreed there was only one course of action.

Ronnie and J. W. went to the studio and loaded up the tapes, every last inch of them, masters and outtakes alike. Mason and I rounded up two pairs of scissors and a butcher knife. Well into the wee hours we unrolled and snipped and hacked and slashed until all that was left of the best damn record ever recorded in Nashville was six plastic garbage bags full of copper-colored confetti. That job done, we hauled the whole load downtown and dumped it off of the Shelby Street bridge, emptying the bags one at a time. As the sun came up we watched true beauty flutter down and settle on the dark, dirty water of the Cumberland River, disappearing around the bend forever.

Take a walk down Music Row. If you drive, you place yourself at the mercy of those one-way streets and you'll only circle down around and back again. You'll see what fits inside your windshield — glass and brick, asphalt and concrete. If you walk you can get down close to the sidewalk, close to where the music is and always has been. Walk slowly and you might even run across an ugly, little flat-roofed, stucco beer joint nearly invisible in the shadow of the giants that have sprung up on both sides. Stop in and have a beer. Take a look around.

Not very impressive, I admit. But hey, give it a chance. Listen to the jukebox. You may hear echoes of what this town once was. Get to know J. W. He's the owner now, since I retired. If he likes you (and if he thinks that you'll get it) he might even play you a tape of a kid from Texas no one ever heard of. Then you'll know what this town could be — if only we deserved it.

THE INTERNATIONALE

THE AMERICAN walked into a coffeehouse in Bergen, Norway, and took a seat at a table just inside the front door. He was tall and gaunt, well over six feet, all angles and shadows with only a trace of gray here and there in his longish dark brown hair and beard to show for his forty-odd years. He wore the expatriate bohemian uniform — jeans, black cotton sweater, denim jacket, and Doc Martens (although cowboy boots were sometimes substituted). He ordered café au lait, lit a cigarette leaving the pack and his lighter out on the table, and surveyed his surroundings as his eyes adjusted to the dim lighting. It was the middle of the day, so there were only a handful of obviously regular patrons in the place. Chet Baker's trumpet drifted from unseen speakers at an almost subliminal volume. A young couple in the back corner argued in hushed tones, creating an invisible perimeter of tension around them, which served to keep would-be eavesdroppers at a comfortable distance. A party of four students with book bags and notebooks in a heap in the center of the table carried on a more lively conversation in Norwegian, chain-smoking and nursing large mugs of coffee. There were two or three other solitary customers scattered here and there around the room. All were of university age and paid little or no attention to the American as he settled in at the small front table — except for one.

The old woman met his gaze head-on, as if she lay there in ambush, watching and waiting as he sized up the room. She sat in the back beside the kitchen door and peered across the room through the cigarette smoke and a faint wisp of steam rising in ringlets from a freshly brewed pot of chamomile tea. She had small, opaque eyes that held his own fast when he attempted to look away. There was that barely perceptible side-to-side shaking of the head that one sometimes observes in the very old, but the eyes never lost track of their target. She was long past the age when even the most astute observer could come within four or five years at a glance. She might have been seventy or well into her eighties but ninety wouldn't have surprised him at all. The waiter who brought her tea called her "mademoiselle" in such a way that it was obvious she was indeed French and the proprietress of this coffeehouse as well.

He began to feel uncomfortable. When he asked for his bill, the waiter cocked his head in the direction of the kitchen door and informed him in near-perfect English that his coffee was on the house with the mademoiselle's compliments. Unable to escape her gaze and feeling obligated now, he crossed the room to thank her. She nodded at the chair across the table from her. He sat down, resigned, but mildly irritated with his inability to decline.

From across the room the mademoiselle was merely old. Up close she was ancient — venerable, even intimidating.

"What brings you to Norway, cheri?"

Despite the familiarity, he suffered that sudden pang in the pit of his stomach that he usually only experienced when he was being interrogated at a border crossing. He framed his answer accordingly — volunteer nothing.

"Vacation," he shrugged.

"Vacation? From what?" She laughed out loud, then quickly

recovered. "Forgive me, cheri. I meant only to ask what you do for a living."

"Oh, I'm in import-export. Curios, crafts, folk art, like that."

Why did I say that? It was none of her fucking business and a little too close to the truth. But she had those lie detector eyes that cut like lasers through subterfuge and innuendo. They reached into his jacket pocket and scanned his meticulously forged passport. They looked inside his mind and ferreted out lies he'd been telling for so many years now that he had begun to believe them himself. Even worse, they saw into his past, which in turn opened a channel to hers. For a moment, through the veil of smoke, he thought he could see her back in Paris. It was the twenties and she was in hers. *God, she must have been somethin'.*

"I know you, cheri."

He winced. She seemed to delight in making him uncomfortable.

"No, no, not *you*, but I've known many men like you."

"And what kind of man am I?"

"My kind, cheri, my kind." She laughed out loud, again. "Relax, relax, I'm far too old for all that now. But once I had a weakness, you could even say an appetite, for adventurers."

"Adventurers?"

"You know, anarchists, mercenaries, smugglers, revolutionaries, writers, poets, painters — which are you, cheri?"

"I told you. I'm only a tourist."

"No, cheri, I see that kind everyday in this place, and you're no tourist. Tourists come through the door with a great commotion and then they usually leave quickly and just as noisily. I guess they think my place isn't Norwegian enough. Every head in the place turns to see what the big noise is all about and they chatter like birds for a while once the intruder is gone. Sometimes it takes the little dears a while to settle down again. But when you came through the door, no one looked up but me."

She summoned the waiter again with a barely perceptible wave of a tiny, almost doll-like hand. The boy bent down low, so she could whisper in his ear. He looked at the American, surprised at first and then impressed. He disappeared into the kitchen.

"I have something special for us tonight, cheri. Something rare. Something definitely not for tourists."

The waiter returned and set an antique pewter tea tray between them on the table. On it were two highball glasses, a sugar bowl, several small utensils the American didn't recognize, and two bottles. One contained the local mineral water. The other was ancient and he couldn't make the label out from where he sat. She nodded and the waiter picked up one of the strange utensils from the tray. It was like a pair of silver sugar tongs but each half was spoon-shaped with multiple perforations like a tea ball. He secured an oblong double sugar cube gently between the antique jaws then picked up an identical device from the tray and repeated the process. He then rested each across the top of a glass, one before the old woman and one before the American, and poured a bright-green liquid from the mysterious old bottle over the sugar cubes, dissolving them before his eyes.

"This is absinthe, cheri, the drink of poets. It has been illegal throughout the world since the turn of the century. They say it drives men mad. This bottle is 120 years old. It was the last of a case kept by the proprietor of a café in Montmartre before the war. When the Germans came, he fled to America and left it with me."

The waiter topped off the glasses with water and then withdrew, leaving the tray.

"To adventurers, cheri."

He drank, obediently.

The bright green of the undiluted liquor gave way to a milky color when the water was added. It tasted of herbs and dust, slightly bitter though not unpleasant. The old woman drank slowly, sensually, never taking her eyes off her guest. After a suitable interval, to allow the absinthe to cast its spell, she lit another cigarette, inhaled deeply, and began her tale in soft, musical tones, her words seemingly borne on tiny puffs of smoke that escaped rhythmically from her nose as she spoke.

"Before the war came, Paris was rotten with adventurers, cheri. They came from all over the world like a plague of locusts. Some came and stayed. Some were merely poseurs. They ordered absinthe in the cafés only to be served cheap anisette without a trace of wormwood. They never knew the difference. The mercenaries and revolutionaries came on their way to or from someplace more exotic, more dangerous. There were little wars then, all over Europe and Asia, wars fought in tiny countries far to the east by ragged peasant armies, led by young idealists. When they were defeated, those who survived fled to Paris while their little bands of peasants rotted in unmarked mass graves. There they fought only tabletop battles in tiny cafés while the more cowardly and gullible among the journalists hung on every word. Some journalists had more balls than others and they went to see this small nightmare firsthand. Some returned, some didn't. Those that did were great lovers, to a man."

The waiter appeared and wordlessly repeated the absinthe ritual. The American's first impulse was to politely refuse but he realized that it was futile and stopped himself. When the waiter withdrew, the mademoiselle continued.

"There were jazz musicians from America, Negroes, cheri. They came only to be treated like men. And we, the ladies of the cafés, obliged them. My girlfriend Natalie knew them all, but many of them used drugs. Opium is a hard mistress, cheri. I do not like the competition.

"I knew all the painters. I modeled for most of them. Not Picasso, though. He only painted women that he loved. Or hated. I'm not sure he knew the difference. I suppose I fell somewhere in between. Just as well. He was a horrible little man, really."

She went on with her monologue in a matter-of-fact manner, dropping name after famous name. Sometimes her tone was judgmental but there was no trace of bitterness and, for some reason he couldn't put his finger on, the American believed every word she said.

"I knew Beckett. Henry Miller, his poor gullible wife, and that whore Anaïs. Hemingway was there, as well as Fitzgerald, Dos Passos, and Gertrude Stein."

A small storm cloud passed over the small, finely chiseled face.

"Never love a writer, cheri, especially a good one. Writers kiss and tell both publicly and privately. Sleep with one and all of his friends will come calling behind his back. Fall in love with one and he will break your heart and then reduce your pain to grist for his typewriter. Then you must live in terror of the day when he is published. Better to love a bad writer who'll take your secrets to his grave. Better still, love a revolutionary. Revolutionaries can keep secrets. They must. It is a matter of life and death to them."

She suddenly stopped and for the first time released the

American from her gaze as she closed her eyes and softly hummed a vaguely familiar tune.

"What's that?"

"That, cheri, is 'The Internationale.' The anthem of the workers of the world."

For the first time he was genuinely intrigued. "Were you a Communist?"

"No, cheri." She smiled, reengaging her one-man audience. "I was a lover of Communists. My older sister was a lover of aviators during the first war. Oh, my poor father. But I had more intellectual tastes. Not that I'm an intellectual myself, cheri. Most of the time I didn't understand what they were going on about. This frustrated the men among them and infuriated the women. But the men were still men. Men of great passion."

She leaned forward as if imparting a great secret.

"It was their passion that attracted me. And mine that drew them to me like bees to clover. It was, shall we say, my own small contribution to the revolution. They were from all over Europe. Germans, English, Italians, Dutch, Spaniards, and there were of course our own French comrades. There were even a few from our own colonies in North Africa and Indochina, but these men kept mostly to themselves. Their revolution was in an active phase as opposed to a rhetorical one. They had no time for diversion. The rest of us drank good cheap wine and coffee and ate day-old bread and lentil soup. At night we talked revolution by candlelight in the cafés and sang 'The Internationale' and then we went home and made love."

The light in her eyes flickered and died. Before the American's eyes she lost her tenuous grip on the Paris of her youth and was dragged back to the present and the little coffeehouse in Norway. She continued but her narrative was somehow flatter, more detached.

"And then the war came. After that nothing was the same. The revolution in Russia was already dead, crushed under the boots of Stalin's death squads and the disease spread across Eastern Europe, borne on the treads of Soviet tanks. In the West the Americans came with their Marshall Plan and their CIA and systematically suffocated every last pocket of true socialism in Europe. Both sides told their people that it was 'Us' against 'Them,' Capitalism versus Communism, Good versus Evil. In truth, they were only two great bullies waging war by proxy in the poor remote corners of the earth while the true socialists rotted in prison or abandoned hope. And now . . . oh well, I knew they were dreaming, cheri. I never really believed."

For the first time all evening her words rang hollow . . . false. The American struggled to conceal his surprise. But the spell was irreparably broken. She rose without a word, grumbling at the waiter in French as he hurried to her side to help. He hurriedly bussed the tea tray and they disappeared into the kitchen leaving the American alone in the café. The other patrons had long since left, so he laid a hundred kroner on the table and got slowly to his feet.

Back out in the street, dark and deserted now that the evening had dissolved like the sugar cube in the mysterious green liqueur, he walked for miles hoping to clear his head, but it was no use. He somehow found his room and lay awake for hours before finally drifting off to sleep.

Even years later, as he wandered the world, a fugitive, unable to ever return home, he still smelled the chamomile and tasted the absinthe and wondered what course his life would have taken had he only been born fifty years earlier. He had been shown a glimpse of a not-so-distant past when lives like his own might have made more sense. A romantic time he'd only just missed of great causes and just wars, when mercenaries and thieves, yes, even smugglers occasionally had the chance to redeem themselves. Sometimes he'd sit for hours over espresso in tiny cafés in obscure little corners of the world, lost in daydreams of a time when adventurers gathered in taverns and held forth long into the night. There they'd drink forbidden potions and spin tales of treasure and triumph in faraway places. And when the bottle was empty and the fire dwindled to orange and black, someone in the darkness would wonder out loud, "What ever happened to 'Red Anna'? You know, the French girl. We once drank absinthe together in Paris before the war."

THE RED SUITCASE

NOTHING LASTS FOREVER. Not even in a small town.

His name was Will'm — or probably William, but his childlike pronunciation of his own given name had stuck with most of the locals over the years. They all called him Will'm and only a few knew his last name or remembered a time when he wasn't a fixture in their town. He had simply always been there, walking up and down Main Street in rapid, choppy little steps, a gait that caused him to wobble comically back and forth as he struggled along with his ever-present suitcases. He always carried two suitcases — one blue and one red — the blue in his right hand and the red in his left. It appeared to the observer that relinquishing his grip on one or the other would surely compromise Will'm's equilibrium sufficiently to capsize him right there in the street.

Nearly everyone Will'm met on his daily trek downtown said "hello," and for his part, Will'm always returned their greeting with a smile no matter how steep the hill or how hot or cold the day. Will'm just kept on wobbling, past the hardware store, past the post office and Freeny's department store. When he reached the county courthouse, at the top of Main Street, he was always pretty well winded, and it would take him a while to catch his breath. He set his suitcases down carefully, bending only at the knees. He had hurt his back once and the nice young doctor at the county hospital had showed him how to lift a heavy load properly. The doctor said that now that Will'm was older he would have to be more careful, and Will'm took the advice to heart, though the "older" part confused him somewhat. Will'm didn't feel older. He understood the concept of aging well enough. He watched as everyone and everything around him grew and aged and changed before his eyes, but he remained the same. He hauled his suitcases up the hill at the same time every morning and then plopped down heavily in the center of a concrete bench and set up shop for the day. There was no need to leave room for anyone else. The bench was Will'm's acknowledged territory from 7:00 A.M. until 5:00 P.M.

First he (carefully) lifted the blue suitcase up onto the bench, opened it, removed a stack of worn comic books (mostly Spiderman, his favorite), and arranged them neatly at one end of the bench. Next he unpacked a neatly creased brown paper bag that contained his lunch — one peanut butter and grape jelly sandwich, one bag of Cheetos, one apple (the red kind, he didn't trust the green ones), and one carton of grape juice with its own little straw attached to the side. Will'm liked grape, or anything else purple for that matter. He had even painted the walls in his little room in the tourist courts a deep lavender he had concocted himself using odds and ends of paint left over from the school Christmas pageant.

When he was satisfied that all was right on his bench, he would just sit and watch the town pass by or read comics until lunchtime was announced by the siren down at the mill. Then, and only then, he would eat his lunch, slowly and deliberately, one item at a time. First the sandwich, then the

Cheetos, then the apple, carefully rationing the grape juice so that he never ran out before his meal was finished. Passersby would greet him and he would smile and nod in response. Only a few actually engaged him in conversation. There was Old Judge Beecher and Mrs. Halley, from the county records office, who brought him baskets of treats on holidays. There was a young lawyer called Thurman Rose. Will'm especially liked Thurman because he often stopped to talk baseball for a while on his way to and from court. Between visits Will'm would read and watch and then read and watch some more. Everyone in town depended on him to simply be there, on his bench, day in and day out. The only constant in their world, and in Will'm's world, was Will'm. Simply being Will'm was his job and he did it well until the siren announced five o'clock.

"Quittin' time!" Will'm would call out. He'd heard it in a movie once a long time ago, and it gave him a great deal of satisfaction to say it at the end of another long day on his bench. Then, carefully and methodically, with the precision and solemnity of a ritual repeated daily for years on end, Will'm packed up his blue suitcase. The red suitcase remained where he had set it down, seemingly forgotten from seven in the morning until "quittin' time," when he hefted it once again for the long walk home.

The trip down the hill was much the same as the trip up, though not nearly as strenuous and somewhat less urgent. Sometimes Will'm would stop and rest on the return trek, though he never set his suitcases down or sat on any of the benches he passed. Will'm was sure that they were someone else's benches and that the proprietor would be along any moment. He just stood there on the sidewalk for a while until his breathing regulated and some of the blood returned to his aching arms and cramped hands, and then he moved along on down the hill.

When the black and white police cruiser imposed itself in Will'm's path at the corner of Main and Elm, Will'm smiled because he assumed that it was Chief Sieler, stopping to chat for a while. Only when Patrolman Gary Huston stepped out of the car did Will'm realize that this officer was a stranger. The big cop grabbed his hat off of the dashboard and pulled it well down on his head, so that the short, patent leather bill almost obscured his eyes. He stood six feet four, and his six years in the Marines had hardened his physique into an imposing angular mass of muscle, spit, and polish. He towered over Will'm, who, stooped by years of hauling his suitcases up and down the hill, appeared even smaller as he cowered in the young officer's shadow.

"My!" said Will'm, "You're a big one."

"Step over to the car, please. Leave the suitcases."

The policeman's brusque manner confused Will'm. In all of his forty-some-odd years, no one had ever spoken to him in that manner, but he knew what to do. He had seen this drill before on those "real life" police programs on TV. To suddenly be a participant rather than a spectator was actually rather exciting. He gingerly set down his precious suitcases and shuffled tentatively past the officer until he was standing by the car, just forward of the open driver's-side door.

There was nothing in Will'm's experience to prepare him for what happened next. Officer Huston removed his nightstick from its hanger on his duty belt and tapped on the hood of the car.

"Put both of your hands right there, on the car."

As Will'm complied the big policeman stepped behind him

and grabbed the waistband of his trousers and yanked hard, pulling them up into Will'm's crotch. He rapped the inside of Will'm's knees, first one and then the other with the nightstick.

"Spread 'em." Pushing Will'm's feet even farther apart with a brisk side-to-side sweeping motion of his own size-thirteen boot, Huston reached around and began fishing in the frightened little man's pockets. "You got anything sharp in your pockets, fella? I'm not gonna get stuck by anything nasty, am I?"

"No, sir. I'm not supposed to have sharp things."

The cop kept rooting around, running his hands up and down Will'm's legs, running his finger around the waistband of his underwear and the tops of his socks.

"Got anything else you ain't supposed to have? Anything you want to tell me about now?"

Will'm thought. He thought hard. He was beginning to sense that answering these questions as accurately as possible was critical. He closed his eyes and concentrated on the possible contents of his pockets — comb, wallet, a pack of gum, a small leather coin purse, and the key to the motel room he had called home for most of his adult life. When he was satisfied that he had thoroughly inventoried everything, he answered the officer's question, but he had begun to stammer slightly, terrified that he had left something out.

"N-no, sir."

Officer Huston grunted his doubt and went on searching Will'm, emptying the contents of his pockets onto the hood of the car. When he was satisfied that Will'm wasn't concealing anything else, he told Will'm to stay where he was and began to rifle through the items on the car. Will'm obediently maintained "the position," his back to the officer so that Huston never saw two large, silent tears slowly sliding down either cheek in near-perfect synchronicity.

Patrolman Huston struggled to maintain his practiced, stern demeanor as he extracted item after item from Will'm's blue suitcase. The process reminded Will'm of a routine he saw in the circus when he was a child, in which no fewer than twenty clowns — big ones, little ones, fat ones, skinny ones — emerged in seemingly endless procession from a single, tiny car. The resulting pile of this and that spread out over the hood of Officer Huston's cruiser appeared far too vast to have ever been contained by the suitcase it had issued from. There were magazines, baseball cards, rubber bands, and bits of string, tinfoil, and copper wire. Will'm collected almost anything that looked useful to him, though his concept of utility was somewhat abstract. There was a glove with no mate, a cheap watch that had stopped forever at precisely 3:17, as well as a stocking cap with a hole in it — they all found sanctuary in Will'm's blue suitcase. They waited silently there under Will'm's care for the long-lost other glove, a battery, or a kind and skillful hand to make them whole again.

Finding no contraband in the blue suitcase, Huston turned his attention toward the red one. Discovering that it was locked, he asked Will'm for the key.

"Key? There ain't no key, sir."

"No key, huh? Well, then how do you open it?"

"Open it?"

"Yeah, open it."

Will'm was confused, even threatened by the very concept. The stammer became more pronounced.

"Uh-h — b-but that's m-my special suitcase, sir. I n-never open that suitcase."

"Well you're damn sure gonna open it now!"

"B-but, sir, I d-don't have the k-key!"

Huston shrugged and reached around to the back of his duty belt and produced a Buck knife, the folding kind with a locking blade. Will'm was reminded of Batman's utility belt but he declined to comment, as he was quietly sobbing by this time and barely able to speak at all.

"In that case I'll just have to open it myself."

"Uh . . . Off-f-ficer?"

The big cop grabbed the red suitcase and swung it up onto the hood of the cruiser in one decisive motion, sweeping the contents of the blue one aside with his free arm.

"Off-ficer, s-sir!"

Huston began to pry at the latch on the red suitcase but his efforts were cut short by an inhuman howl that seemed to issue from somewhere deep inside of Will'm.

"No-o-o-o! Stop!"

The patrolman froze but he wasn't sure exactly why. He stared at Will'm, who seemed to have suddenly found a new voice and lucidity that demanded his attention. Even the stammer had disappeared.

"Don't you have to have a warrant for that, sir?"

A warrant? The mere suggestion would have been more than enough to buy Will'm a trip downtown in the back of Huston's cruiser had Chief Sieler not stumbled onto the scene on his way home from work.

"Huston! What the Sam Hill do you think you're doing?"

"Oh, how you doin' there, Chief? . . . Uh-h-h, Chief, the subject here was observed loitering around the neighborhood. I stopped him and asked to see what he was carrying in these suitcases here and he —"

"That's no subject, you moron, that's Will'm!"

Walking around to the front of Huston's cruiser, Chief Sieler patted Will'm on the shoulder reassuringly like a mother comforting an embarrassed child.

"Will'm, you all right?"

Chief Sieler had known Will'm since he was a small boy. He had known Will'm's mother as well. In fact, he had arrested her on several occasions for petty infractions — prostitution, public drunkenness, or the odd minor drug charge. When she was found dead of old age at forty-eight, Will'm, all of ten at the time, was made a ward of the state and housed in the county hospital's psychiatric unit. The chief and Judge Beecher, who had signed the order remanding Will'm into state custody, looked in on Will'm from time to time. As he grew in years and size, and years and size only, the two men brought him gifts of gadgets and comic books on his birthday and Christmas. On his eighteenth birthday, when the latest social worker assigned to Will'm's case announced that Will'm would have to leave the county hospital, the chief made a few phone calls and arranged for Will'm to receive a small check from the state. Will'm also recieved a hundred dollars worth of food stamps every month and placement in Section Eight subsidized housing — the little motel room.

Oddly, it was the same compassion and philanthropic spirit that had driven Chief Sieler to hire the son of his wife's sister, fresh from the Marine Corps, sight unseen. Gary Huston had learned everything he knew about police work while serving as an MP, and he was known for his encyclopedic knowledge of the regulations. He was on the waiting list for the police academy in Detroit, where he grew up, but his military experience alone qualified him for a spot on most small-town police forces. He had been on the job for just over two months, most of which he spent behind a desk or riding along with a senior officer. Now that he was out on the streets in a cruiser of his own, he wasn't disposed to tolerate vagrancy or loitering. He had simply never seen Will'm before and had no way of knowing that he was something of an institution around town. He was also known for an absolute inability to admit that he was wrong, under any circumstances.

"Chief, the subject — uh, I mean Will'm here — refuses to open this here red suitcase. Now, you know as well as I do that I don't need a warrant to search a subject's person. It's a matter of my own safety, and you know better than me that an officer's safety comes first on the street."

"Safety? What the Sam Hill are you talking about, Gary? I've known this boy for over thirty years. He's no threat to you or anybody else!"

"But, Chief, he can't just *refuse* to open that suitcase, just like that. I'm a duly appointed officer of the law, and departmental procedure clearly states that an officer's determination that his safety may be at stake constitutes probable cause for a thorough search of the subject's person for weapons and or contraband — at the officer's discretion."

"Weapons? Will'm hasn't got any weapons in there. Do you, Will'm? Any weapon's in there, son?" Will'm probably would have innocently answered the rhetorical question but the chief didn't give him time. "See, what'd I tell you. Besides, it looks to me like you've already searched his person pretty thoroughly and this other suitcase here as well."

"Well, Chief, the — Will'm here — consented to the search of the blue suitcase. He didn't get uncooperative until I asked to see what was in that red one there. Don't you find that just a little bit suspicious?"

"Suspicious? Now look here, Huston. You're new around here. When you've been around for a while you'll know that there is nothing suspicious about Will'm or his suitcases. He was haulin' 'em up Main Street, to that same bench in front of the courthouse before you were born."

A light, however dim, ignited in Officer Huston's eyes.

"The courthouse? A government building? Don't you see, Chief? What if there was a bomb in that suitcase?"

"A bomb? Fercrissakes, Huston! A bomb! And I suppose you believe that Will'm has been draggin' that suitcase up and down the longest, steepest hill in the county everyday, for as long as anyone around here can remember, with a bomb in it waiting for — what? The Rapture? Will'm?"

"Y-yes, sir?"

"You got a bomb in that suitcase, son?"

"I don't know, sir."

"See, Huston, what'd I tell you —"

Will'm's reply was slow in sinking in. By the time the chief realized what had actually been said, Officer Huston had drawn his sidearm and was demanding that Will'm "step away from the suitcase."

"Huston, put that damn thing up this instant, or I'll send you packing back to Detroit, never you mind who your mama is." He turned his attention back to Will'm. His tone was gentle and only slightly condescending. "Will'm, son, what do you mean, 'you don't know'?"

Will'm shuffled his feet nervously and stared at the ground.

"I m-mean I d-don't know, sir. I mean I n-never open that suitcase. I n-never *have* opened that suitcase. It was locked when I found it."

Naturally, Huston seized on this latest information as even more "probable cause." "What if it contains stolen property?" he challenged.

The chief held Huston in check with an irritated sidelong glare.

"Will'm, where, exactly, did you find the red suitcase, son?"

The answer would have to wait. A crowd of curious citizens had begun to gather, and as if that wasn't enough, the county's newly formed bomb squad and half of the Fire Department had arrived on the scene.

"Oh fercrissakes, Huston!"

The chief grabbed the red suitcase in one hand and Will'm's sleeve in the other and shepherded them into his car, leaving Officer Huston and the bomb squad and the Fire Department boys milling around in the middle of Elm Street looking and feeling more than a little foolish.

During the ride downtown Will'm calmed down enough to tell the chief how he'd found the red suitcase in a dumpster behind the bus station more than twenty years ago. According to Will'm, apart from being a little redder and a lot less battered, the suitcase had been in, more or less, the same condition when he found it — locked. He had never attempted to open it. When asked why, he would only repeat that the red suitcase was his "special suitcase" and that he never opened it. After traveling a block or two, Will'm seemed to be more interested in all the gadgets in the chief's cruiser. He asked the chief to crank up the siren and the flashing blue lights on the dashboard, and the chief, as usual, indulged him. The townspeople stopped and stared as the cruiser passed, and Will'm waved from the back seat like a visiting dignitary riding at the head of a motorcade.

Thurman Rose strode unannounced into Judge Beecher's chambers, ignoring Chief Sieler, Mrs. Halley, and the half-dozen other assorted city employees that were standing around. Will'm's face immediately brightened when he recognized the young attorney, but he kept his seat in the old oaken office chair. Thurman dropped to one knee and addressed Will'm directly, as he did nearly every day when he visited Will'm at his bench out front. Will'm liked that. It made him feel grown up. Everyone else invariably stood over him making him feel small and insignificant. But Thurman always engaged Will'm eye to eye, one baseball fan to another.

"Hey buddy, how you doin' there?"

"Oh, I'm all right. Did you see me, Thurman? The chief turned on the siren and the lights and we rode right down Main Street."

"Yeah, I saw you, buddy. Everybody saw you. You looked great."

Thurman glanced around the room trying to sort the situation out. He was careful not to say too much in front of Will'm until he knew what was going on. The first thing he noticed was that everyone present looked a little sheepish, as if they were somewhat uncomfortable with the proceedings. They all stopped talking when he came in and most avoided eye contact with Thurman as he looked from face to face, searching for some hint of what was taking place. The centerpiece of the whole odd scenario was Will'm's red suitcase sitting, still unopened, in the middle of Judge Beecher's judge-sized oak desk. The prominent position lent the otherwise ordinary-looking suitcase an air of importance, like a rare artifact in a museum.

"So what's goin' on here, buddy?"

Will'm surveyed the room himself, as if trying to determine if it was safe to talk. He motioned for Thurman to come closer and whispered in his ear.

"They want to open my suitcase. Thurman, you're a lawyer.

They can't open my suitcase, can they? I mean, without a warrant, or something?"

Thurman glanced at the suitcase in its place of honor on the desk. "Well, Will'm, I don't know. That depends. Tell me, buddy, has anyone told you why they want to open your suitcase?"

Will'm was still whispering. "They think there's a bomb in it."

"A bomb! Why that's silly. Well, why don't you just open it and show them that there's no bomb in there."

Will'm spoke out loud this time, his jaw set in a determined grimace. "No!"

"Well, why not?"

"Because that's my special suitcase. I never, ever open that suitcase."

Now Thurman was whispering. "Well, is there anything in your suitcase that I should know about? I mean as your attorney?"

Will'm drew a long breath and let it go, making a soft whistling sound through his teeth. "You mean you're my lawyer, Thurman?"

"Yeah, I mean, if you want me to be."

"Oh! I think that would be wonderful! But —" Will'm looked confused, the faint lines in his forehead contracting into deep creases as his smile melted away. "Oh my, Thurman. I must be in a lot of trouble."

"No, buddy, you're not in trouble. Just a bit of a misunderstanding. But I do need to know, as your attorney, I mean — what's in your suitcase?"

Will'm scanned the room once more. Everyone *was* listening now. He grabbed the lapels of Thurman's coat and pulled him closer, whispering even softer than before.

"I told them. I don't know. I never, ever open that suitcase."

Thurman searched Will'm's eyes and found nothing to dissuade him from taking everything he had been told at face value, just as he always did. In fact, what Thurman had always liked most about Will'm was his honesty, his absolute incapacity for guile. With Will'm, unlike almost everyone else in the world, Thurman always knew where he stood.

"OK, buddy, you wait right here and try not to worry. Everything will be all right."

Thurman located Chief Sieler in his peripheral vision and subtly gestured toward the door behind him with a sideways motion of his head. "Chief, could I talk to you for a minute? Excuse us, please, Will'm."

Thurman and the chief stepped out into the hall followed by Officer Huston, who had just arrived at the courthouse out of breath and humiliated. Thurman had never seen the young cop before.

"Excuse me, Officer — uh-h —" Thurman glanced down at the stranger's nametag. "— Huston is it? I was speaking to the chief."

The chief, realizing for the first time that he had acquired a shadow, visibly bristled. "Fercrissake, Huston! Give us a minute here!"

"Now Chief, I am the arresting officer and departmental procedure clearly states —"

Thurman cut him off in mid-regulation. He addressed the chief, barely acknowledging Huston's existence. "Arresting officer? So, Will'm's under arrest, then?"

"No, no, not exactly — we just want to talk with Will'm about his suitcase."

"Well Chief, he's either under arrest or he's not. If he's not, then it's way past supper time, and I think we can all go home now. If he is —"

Huston desperately interjected, like a neglected younger sibling in a family argument. "Now I don't know who you think you are there, fella, but this here is police business —"

Thurman and the chief turned on Huston simultaneously, their heads rotating in perfect sync, wordlessly silencing the frustrated officer as Thurman continued: "— and if Will'm is under arrest, then I am his attorney, and if you need to talk to Will'm about his suitcase, or anything else for that matter, then the person you need to be talking to is me."

"His attorney? Since when?"

"Since Will'm said I was."

The chief was bothered, not so much by the revelation itself as the cumulative effect of the afternoon's events. This was starting to get complicated. Far more complicated than life had any business being in a small town.

"Well, Will'm's not under arrest."

"Then he's free to go."

"Well, not exactly. It's just that Huston here, as much as I hate to admit it, has a point. He may have been well within his rights as a peace officer asking Will'm to open his suitcase and, well, I'm no lawyer but . . . Now be honest, Thurman. Haven't you ever wondered about the *red* suitcase? How he only opens the blue suitcase and never the red one? You have to admit, it's pretty dern strange. Anyhow, Judge Beecher is on the way in now. We'll sort it all out when he gets here."

Nothing lasts forever. No place. No time. No routine. Not even in a small town. We, the citizens, would like to believe that we leave behind a perpetual ritual of some kind, a template for our children and theirs — our own little collective bid for mortality. We want to believe that our traditions endure, perhaps because life itself is so fleeting. But it simply isn't so. Cycles, in time, run their course, to be replaced by new, improved ones. Most of us live out our lives in between the parentheses, our existence comfortably enclosed within the confines of a clear-cut epoch. But once in a while, for an unfortunate few of us, everything changes *on our watch*. One piece of the pyramid we have carefully constructed for generation upon generation is yanked unceremoniously from the bottom of the pile and nothing is ever the same again, clearing the decks and setting the stage for something totally unexpected.

Judge Beecher arrived a little past eight, sporting a seldom-worn tuxedo he had squeezed himself into for the fall soiree at the country club. The truth be told, he was relieved when he received the phone call from Chief Sieler just as he and his wife were about to walk out the door, but he felt a need to maintain appearances.

"Chief, this better be good."

The chief apologized and then proceeded to relate the evening's events. Mrs. Halley brought coffee, and the judge settled into his massive, black leather chair, visibly irritated at the presence of Will'm's red suitcase in the center of his meticulously organized desk. The chief accepted a cup as well, barely acknowledging the hospitality as he concentrated on presenting the facts accurately and in chronological order. He was interrupted about the time he reached the part about the bomb squad by Officer Huston, who could no longer contain himself. There ensued a deluge of state and city codes as well as departmental procedure, all accurately quoted, if not exactly relevant to the matter at hand. Suddenly the proceedings degenerated into bedlam, everyone speaking at once — everyone, that is, except Will'm, who sat quietly in his chair staring at one tiny area of the dusty Oriental rug between his feet.

Normally at times like this, when "grownups" talked about grown-up things, Will'm went into a kind of trance. The conversation around him would dissolve into a distant, familiar hum, like an air conditioner or a ceiling fan, lulling Will'm into a low emotional idle. The state resembled catatonia, but in reality it was a discipline of sorts, allowing Will'm to weather the torrent of dense language swirling around him without feeling overwhelmed. But tonight the grownups were talking about Will'm. Just when he would settle into that safe space in his head, he would hear his name mentioned again, rudely dragging him back into conciousness. Officer Huston said that Will'm had "a history of mental illness." Chief Sieler retorted that was ridiculous. Will'm, he insisted, wasn't "crazy, just a little bit slow." Even Thurman was talking about him as if he wasn't in the room in big words that Will'm didn't understand. Something about "an unlawful search" and someone called Miranda, whom Will'm had never heard of.

Judge Beecher sat behind his desk, poring over a huge, dusty book of constitutional law offering only an occasional grunt or "hmm." Even he was oblivious, completely absorbed, like everyone else in the room, in his own little part of the drama, when Will'm suddenly and silently stood up and started across the room in short, choppy steps. With each step Will'm gained confidence. Suddenly, he felt powerful. Instead of feeling ignored, he felt — invisible. As he wobbled, still unnoticed, right up to the big desk, he tugged at the piece of purple yarn around his neck, pulling the key that hung suspended there, out from its hiding place beneath his shirt. His secret. His only secret. The impetus for the only lie that he had ever

told in his life. And he had told it twice, once to Officer
Huston and once to Thurman. Well, no matter. He knew what
to do. His hand trembled as he, still unnoticed, placed the tiny
key into the latch, closed his eyes, took one last deep breath,
and then turned the key. Will'm winced as the latch opened
with a sharp click, silencing the roar around him.

Everyone had stopped talking. Will'm no longer felt invisible. In fact, all eyes were on him but it was OK now. His eyes
still shut tight, he reached out until he felt his hands grasping
either side of the suitcase and gently lifted the lid.

They were going to open the suitcase anyway, despite anything Will'm could do or Thurman could say. They had already made up their minds and were merely going through the
formalities now. It was only a matter of time before the judge,
with much apologetic rhetoric about the law and his responsibility to the community, would give the go-ahead and Huston
would pry open the latch with his Buck knife, a smirk on
his whiskerless face. Will'm could see that clearer than he
had seen anything in all of his life. The truth be told, even
Thurman was dying to know what was in the red suitcase. The
one and only thing that remained in Will'm's control was the
decision to open it, himself. Now, standing before the judge's
desk, in that breathless instant before he opened his eyes,
Will'm felt a power, his power, and the power of the suitcase,
drawing everyone in the room close around him. Straining
their necks and standing on tiptoes, they peered over Will'm's
shoulder to see that the red suitcase was empty.

"Oh my," intoned Will'm. "That's what I was afraid of."

Chief Sieler drove Will'm home through the dark streets of
the town, past the post office, past the hardware store, past
Freeny's, and he, Will'm, and the cruiser's siren were deaf-

eningly silent for the entire trip. When they reached the tourist courts, Will'm opened his door and got out without a word, hauling the blue suitcase out of the back seat and starting for his room. Halfway across the courtyard, he stopped when the chief honked his horn and rolled down the passenger-side window to shout.

"Will'm! What about the red suitcase?"

Will'm looked down at the blue suitcase and then at the empty, open palm of his left hand.

"Aw, you just keep it, Chief. There ain't nothin' in that suitcase anyway." Will'm disappeared into the motel room, shutting the door behind him.

The chief took a roundabout route home, a habit of his when he was troubled. He found it reassuring to ride through the streets of his hometown after most people were already safely in their beds. It made him feel like a guardian angel watching over the town while it slept. But tonight, no matter how long he drove around in circles, he still felt unsettled. There was something in the air, a kind of tension as if there was a cold snap or a storm coming. Finally he drove home.

The first thing the chief did on Monday was fire Gary Huston. He gave no reason and Huston didn't ask for one. He just emptied his locker and caught the next bus back to Detroit. Eight months later the chief suffered a mild stroke and retired from the force. He could be seen out at the lake from time to time fishing, but he seldom came to town.

A year and a half after that, Judge Beecher retired to Florida. He died there years later, eight days short of his eightieth birthday.

Thurman Rose went on to become the district attorney and eventually was elected judge, occupying Judge Beecher's old chambers in the courthouse. That is, until the county built a modern office building out on the bypass next to the new Wal-Mart.

The courthouse was never quite the same without Will'm anyway. He never made the long walk up the hill again. Instead, he spent his days in his room reading his comics and watching TV until one night when he simply disappeared. No one could say where he went or why. His bench sat, unpainted and neglected, like everything else downtown, until eventually the city dismantled it and hauled it away to prevent members of the growing homeless population from sleeping on it. When the mill shut down, people moved away in droves, and the old-timers feared the town would die. Instead, it only hollowed out from the center, an empty space where its very heart had been. The Wal-Mart itself sucked what life was left from the businesses along Main Street, and one by one they closed their doors. The empty storefronts and boarded-up windows stared out like sightless eyes on nearly empty streets that only a generation before bustled with men, women, and children going about the everyday business of living their lives.

But nothing lasts forever. Not even in a small town.

A EULOGY OF SORTS

HAROLD MILLS died last night, alone in his $75-a-week room at the Drake Motel, and I'm probably the only motherfucker on Murfreesboro Road that misses him. Hell, I'm the only one that knows he's gone. I just happened to pull up in front of his room just as the EMTs carried him out with a sheet over his face. I had intended to use his place to shoot a couple of pills and cook up an eightball of coke I'd just bought, but I guess I was a little late. On another night he probably would've laid there on the bathroom floor for days until the smell alerted the manager. As it was, the couple next door was interrupted in mid-stroke by a loud bang, which as it turns out was Harold's big ol' head smashing into the tub as he went down. The crushing blow to the back of his skull alone could've easily killed him, but I'd be willing to bet Harold was dead before he hit the floor.

Junkies die down here everyday. Most of the time nobody notices but other junkies, and they perceive only a brief interruption in the food chain. Nobody down here is really capable of mourning in the normal sense. Oh, we suffer the inconvenience of losing a connection, or a safe place to get high or scam a new set of works or maybe crash for a few hours, but that's about it. As unnerving as life in this neighborhood may appear to the uninitiated, we, the wraiths who inhabit its dark-

est corners, find each day even more numbingly boring than
the one before. But that's cool. We hate surprises. Any break in
the tedium makes us uncomfortable. You see, all junkies travel
in ever-narrowing concentric circles until the day they find
themselves running for their lives with one foot nailed to the
floor, as the Beast bears down on them. Grieving over another
dope fiend finally, inevitably running out of luck is simply a
luxury nobody on the pike can afford, because all of us know
that but for the grace of God . . . well hell, there ain't no grace
down here. It's just a matter of time.

So when Harold's time finally ran out, I wasn't there. Not
that I could've saved him anyway. Harold didn't die of an
overdose per se. He most likely had a heart attack that was
coming anyway, no matter what the coroner's report says. Ol'
Harold merely expedited matters with one long, final pull on
his meticulously maintained glass pipe. The pathologist on
duty probably never looked any further than the painfully thin,
needle-scarred arms before rendering Harold's entire life down
into homogeneous statistic.

When I first met Harold Mills he was a real player, the biggest Dilaudid dealer in South Nashville. Dilaudid is the trade
name for hydromorphone hydrochloride, a pharmaceutical
narcotic typically prescribed only for terminal cancer patients.
Nashville, located smack-dab in the middle of the most land-
locked state in the Union, has never enjoyed a particularly dependable heroin supply. Then in the seventies two brothers
by the name of Mitchell from North Nashville's middle-class
black community began to bring in Dilaudid, misappropriated
from drug wholesalers in Detroit and Chicago. A good supply
of relatively cheap, strong heroin kept the price of the pharmaceutical drug low in major northern cities, but in Nashville the
tiny yellow pills brought between forty and sixty dollars each

on the street. In a market where an addict could spend nearly that amount on a bag of highly diluted, low-grade Mexican heroin, "D's" were an instant hit. Harold, being related by marriage to the Mitchell brothers, was in on the ground floor.

The first time I saw Harold he was slow-draggin' Lewis Street in a sky-blue 1978 Cadillac sedan DeVille. He was dressed sharp in an old-school, super-fly, dope-dealer-with-a-heart-of-gold-and-a-tooth-to-match kind of way. He draped his slight six-feet-two frame across the entire front seat as he leaned across to eye me suspiciously through the passenger-side window. I was being introduced by a coke dealer named Clarence Brown. Make no mistake, South Nashville was *about* cocaine. By this point in my career as a lifelong dope fiend, I had taken to smoking several hundred dollars worth of rock cocaine everyday. Coke was a drug I had never particularly cared for. By this time, however, my tolerance for opiates had become prohibitively high, so I took up the practice of "speed-balling," that is, adding a little coke to my frequent injections of Dilaudid for a little extra kick. Exposing myself to cocaine opened the door to freebasing — mixing the deadly white powder with baking soda and cooking it down into smokable "rock" (or "crack" on the East Coast). One hit, crossing my eyes to watch the opaque white smoke billow and expand in the glass bowl and then disappear like a flirtatious genie as I removed my finger from the carburetor and inhaled deeply, and it was a wrap.

No drug had ever grabbed ahold of me as quickly or held me as tightly in its grip. I became conditioned, like some space-race laboratory monkey, to keep pushing that button, too far gone to give a fuck whether I received a banana-flavored pellet or a 110-volt shock. I'd drive to the projects in East Nashville every morning and buy a pill or two, and as soon as I was straight, head down south to Clarence's to smoke. By five or six in the evening, I was getting sick again, so I'd slide back across the river to cop a few more pills, then back across the bridge and — what did the directions say? Repeat if necessary? Well, it was always necessary as a motherfucker. Clarence had only recently given up on trying to "help" me kick Dilaudid. He saw my other habit as a waste of money I could be spending on coke, his personal drug of choice. When he finally got it through his head that that wasn't ever going to happen, he introduced me to Harold Mills, the only hustler down South who regularly traded in Dilaudid. To Clarence this was simply a means to an end: keeping one of his best customers on his side of the river where he could keep his eye on me. Harold listened while Clarence vouched for me, looked me over one more time and then there was a sudden flash as he bared that big, gold front tooth in an ear-to-ear grin. "I heard about you. I heard you spend money."

He sold me a pill (at $10 less than I was paying for singles out East) and scribbled his beeper number on the dismembered top of a hard pack of Kools, promising to cut me a better price when I bought more than one.

I began seeing Harold twice a day, everyday, once in the morning and once just before dark. I knew better than to try and procure a whole day's supply of dope in one run. That kind of thinking only led to a bigger, even more expensive habit, and God knows I was capable of shooting as many pills at one sitting as I could buy. At first I'd just beep him and he'd meet me somewhere up on the pike. After he got to know me better, he gave me his home number, and I would call to make sure he was home before driving to his apartment in the projects where he lived with his wife Keena and their three boys, ages three, four, and seven. I'd do my wake-up shot right there in Harold's bathroom, and then we'd sit around for a while, watching Oprah and shit on the tube and play with the kids. Harold taught his oldest boy, Courtney, to call me Uncle Honky. He thought that shit was hilarious. In the course of those long dreamlike mornings I found out what I should have already known: Harold sold Dilaudid because Harold shot Dilaudid — lots of it. I was a good customer. Most addicts couldn't afford the kind of volume I bought everyday. Harold was beginning to get "hot" on the street, which meant that every time he rolled out on the pike he ran the risk of being stopped on sight by one of the neighborhood patrol cars or even the vice squad. My business meant Harold could support his own habit without taking so many chances.

We quickly fell into a daily routine of getting high together and solving all the world's problems by the time Keena got home from work. We'd engage in long animated discussions on politics (Harold styled himself a Democrat but he reckoned I was probably a Communist), music (we both loved the old Memphis stuff but I knew more about hip-hop than he did, which he didn't care for any more than "that hillbilly shit ya'll listen to"), even the existence of God (I didn't believe in God, Harold did; he just figured that God didn't mess with junkies one way or the other). Never mind that neither of us had voted, bought records, nor been to church in years. Oh yeah, we knew we were addicts. We even referred to ourselves and each other as "junkies." "You a junkie motherfucker." "Well you a junkie, too." Then we'd laugh our asses off. But god forbid a "citizen" ever calls us that. "Junkie" is a funny word like that. It's kind of like "nigger," I guess.

Harold, like me, was a fairly nontypical dope fiend. He still had a family, a place to live, a car, food to eat. Our common ground, it turned out, was that most of the catastrophes that

punctuate "those other" junkies' lives hadn't happened to us
. . . yet. You see, we were both smart enough to know our luck
couldn't hold out forever, so I guess we had just decided to
stick together for a while and wait for the other shoe to drop.

And drop it did. I finally lost touch with Harold a few years
later when I migrated to Los Angeles in my never-ending quest
for stronger and cheaper dope. In the shape I was in, it didn't
take me very long to wear out my welcome in L.A., and eigh-
teen months later, I was back on the pike asking around about
Harold Mills. Some folks said he was locked up. "Naw, he out
East living with his auntie." There was even a story that Harold
had AIDS.

When I finally tracked him down, I immediately saw where
the AIDS rumors came from. Harold was always thin, but now
he was nothing but sallow, translucent skin, stretched taut over
brittle bone. He was wearing a faded, threadbare sweat suit
and run-over Kmart sneakers, shit he would never have been
caught dead in a year earlier. His usually close-cropped hair
was grown out and matted from months of scuffling up and
down the pike, hustling for hits. When he recognized me, he
smiled, revealing that even the trademark gold tooth was missing along with several of his own. But it wasn't AIDS that had
taken Harold down through there. It was rock cocaine.

In all the time I'd known him, I'd never seen Harold Mills
touch crack. I use to have to listen to him and Clarence,
the coke man, one in one ear and one in the other, like those
little guys that sit on a motherfucker's shoulders in the car-
toons, one admonishing him to do the right thing and one
leading him astray. Only, in my cartoon they were *both* devils.
Harold used to say, "That shit was sent by Satan his self to finish the dope fiends off." Now the Beast had him by the balls,
and he knew it. On top of that, his heart had been weakened

by endocarditis, an infection of the bloodstream common to IV drug users. Harold's deterioration in such a short amount of time was especially unsettling to me. After all, he was the same kind of junkie I was. Seeing him like this was too much like looking in a mirror and being confronted by my own death staring back at me through hollow sockets. But after an awkward instant we exchanged dope fiend pleasantries, drove across the river, bought six pills at an exorbitant price, and retired to the Drake Motel to get high. I rented Harold a room there, where he lived for the rest of his life . . . about seven months.

Harold Mills will be buried tomorrow in Greenwood Cemetery in South Nashville. The funeral will cost his grandmother, who raised him, her entire life savings. She rarely saw Harold the last few years of his life. He'd appear on her doorstep now and then, and she'd give him $20 and watch helplessly as he faded back into the night. Then she'd cry herself to sleep. She never once turned him away, even though she knew what he did with the money. She was just thankful that he loved her enough not to come around too often.

Harold will go down to Greenwood decked out in a new blue suit and surrounded by his wife, his kids, and several relatives, mostly older, who haven't seen him since he was a child. Good, solid, working folks who never knew the hustler, the junkie, the derelict. Never saw him sitting in the back seat of a police car in handcuffs or led into a courtroom dressed in a blaze-orange jumpsuit. Never had to watch in horror, as he mined scar tissue–armored veins for the nearly always empty promise of blood commingling with morphine, just before he pushed it back into his ravaged body and waited for the rush that never quite lived up to that sacred memory of his very first hit.

Most of these folks never knew that Harold Mills. They'll come to Greenwood to bury a husband, a daddy, a grandson, and a little boy who used to ride his tricycle through their flower beds.

I won't be there to say goodbye. None of us, the creatures that knew Harold out here on the pike, will be there, because funerals, they say, are for the living . . . and we're already dead. We're just waiting our turn.

See you when I get there, brother.

THE REUNION

There is an American at the Caravelle Hotel in Ho Chi Minh City. The management has asked him to leave. He refuses. Come at once.

Nguyen read and reread the message from General Cao. *How odd*, he thought. Surely an unruly tourist, even an American, is a matter for the local police, not the army. After all, he was on leave, his first in more than two years. He wasn't due to report back to his post in the Army Public Information Office in Ho Chi Minh City for another eleven days yet, and he and his wife were just beginning to settle into the rhythm of a long overdue vacation. They had spent the first week with their daughter in Da Nang, where he held his grandson for the very first time. From there they backtracked south to the resort city of Nha Trang. They had scrimped and saved for twenty years for this trip. The new hotels on the beach were built to attract foreign tourists and were out of the reach of most Vietnamese, especially soldiers, but veterans of the American War were eligible for a small discount, and his wife, Tranh, had her heart set on it. She was luxuriating on the beach now, sipping fresh coconut milk from the shell and marveling at all of the different sorts of people who had traveled thousands of miles from places she had only read or dreamed about. They wore the latest fashions from Europe and spoke odd languages, some coarse and unmusical to her ear. Still she found the strangers fascinating. It would break her heart when she learned that Nguyen would have to return to Ho Chi Minh immediately. But the general was explicit, and Nguyen was a soldier in the Army of the Socialist Republic of Vietnam. He broke the news to Tranh and caught the first train to Ho Chi Minh City.

All the way to Ho Chi Minh, Nguyen stared out the window as the country that he had fought to liberate from the Americans passed by — brilliant green, meticulously tended rice fields, and oddly misshapen jungle-draped mountains. In the fifties his uncles had fought in those very mountains with Uncle Ho, and his father had died far from his home in Ben Duoc, guillotined by the French in the prison that American POWs would later dub the Hanoi Hilton. His mother's father died face down in a rice paddy in Quang Tri province resisting the Japanese invasion, and some of his ancestors had fought the Chinese. Vietnam was always being invaded by someone or other, but she had never been truly conquered. Nguyen's family had always been at the center of the struggle, a proud tradition stretching back a thousand years. But Nguyen's war had been fought entirely against the Americans, in and around his native Cu Chi district.

"Colonel Nguyen, I am told you speak fluent English."

General Cao was from the North and he had served with General Giap, the genius himself. He was in his late sixties, thin and weathered, his sallow, battle-scarred skin stretched taut as a bowstring over bones that had been shattered by both French and American bullets. The old man was one of the last of his kind — a real revolutionary hero who had fought the French, and in these times a bit of an anachronism. He looked uncomfortable behind his desk, chain-smoking Lucky

Strikes and nervously opening and closing his Zippo, keeping it handy to light the next one.

Nguyen set down his teacup and answered in the even, measured tones that he had learned instilled confidence in superiors and subordinates alike.

"I was a guerrilla operative during the war, General. I worked at many jobs for the enemy — houseboy, cook, driver. I gathered information and reported to my cell leader in Cu Chi. I suppose I have an aptitude for languages — I also speak French, Cantonese, Khmer, and some Russian."

"Well, it is your English that we need here today, Colonel, as well as all the diplomacy and discretion you can muster. All we know about this man is that he is an American, that he arrived from Cambodia overland three weeks ago, that the passport he is traveling with is a forgery, his name fictitious — and that he has a gun."

Nguyen showed no outward surprise, his officers' training serving him well.

"He has asked specifically to speak with an army officer who speaks English. He is fortunate that the police colonel who received the call from the hotel manager was a Party member and intelligent enough to know that the Leadership would be very upset if anything unfortunate involving an American were to develop — at least until we know more about this man. There are political considerations."

"I understand, General. You may depend on me."

Training again. Inwardly, he didn't share the general's confidence in his suitability to this assignment, but that was far from apparent. He finished his tea, saluted the general, and strode confidently into the street. He hailed a "cyclo," a kind of combination tricycle and rickshaw powered by its driver.

"The Caravelle Hotel."

The driver pedaled effortlessly across three lanes of traffic in a wide arch and down the busy boulevard.

The American sat up in bed, propped up on a mountain of soft feather pillows. Quite an improvement, he noted, over the Caravelle he periodically terrorized during the war. The old hotel in downtown Ho Chi Minh had been recently renovated. Gone was all of the shabby, painted-over French Provincial furniture, replaced by tasteful reproductions. Cool, dry air whispered down in delicious waves from a modern central air-conditioning system, replacing the old ceiling fans, which never seemed to do much besides stir the stifling atmosphere around a little, like a hot, viscous soup. There was even cable television, complete with a remote to scan through the channels and a mute feature. For the first few days he had surfed up and down the channels in a trancelike, morphine-induced haze, half-watching the news on CNN or a soccer match on one of the sports channels. After about a week he settled on MTV, though he rarely turned the sound up. Even when he did, he never listened to an entire song, just enough to satisfy his curiosity and then he would hit the mute button, once again.

The pain in his back was beginning to nag at him, but he elected to wait as long as he could, as the supply of morphine sulfate tablets the doctor in Amsterdam had prescribed was running low. He was trying to find a comfortable position, leaning awkwardly and painfully forward while fumbling with the pillows behind his back when his hand fell on something hard and cold. The gun.

He had bought the old Russian pistol from a policeman three weeks earlier in Cambodia. The government over there hadn't paid the army or the national police in something like three months, and policemen gathered around all of the tourist attractions, such as the famous temples in Siem Reep province, offering their badges for sale as souvenirs for five dollars, U.S. One persistent officer followed him into one of the makeshift open-air cafés outside the entrance to Angkor Wat and, after looking both ways and lowering his voice to a hissing whisper, offered him the weapon for twenty bucks. For some reason the American bought it. He had traveled all over the world, mostly in "third world" countries, and he had learned long ago that the authorities in places like this didn't take kindly to foreigners going around armed. But nowadays, since a young Dutch doctor had matter-of-factly passed his death sentence, he simply didn't give a fuck. At the time he thought it might even come in handy, if the pain became unbearable.

He hauled the heavy pistol out from its hiding place under the pillow once again and cradled it in both hands, his finger on the scored trigger and his thumb resting on the safety catch. He tilted his head back until it rested against the headboard behind him, closed his eyes, and pressed the cold muzzle against the soft flesh under his chin. He could almost feel the bullet smashing through the roof of his mouth and exiting the top of his head in a shower of bone and blood, carrying half his brain and the cancer that was eating him alive along with it. He simply couldn't bring himself to thumb off the safety and get it over with. Nerve was not the issue. He had never suffered a shortage of that commodity. Since the war the American had been a bush pilot, a smuggler, even an unwitting CIA operative. He had spent the past ten years as a fugitive, traveling light in the murky margins of the world, engaging few and trusting no one.

The knock on the door delayed the deliberations.

"Mr. Engle? May I come in?"

Nguyen called through the hotel room door in flawless English, but he stumbled over the pronunciation of the American's name as recorded on the hotel registration card. He couldn't get his tongue around the "L," situated as it was in the beginning of the second syllable, so it came out "Inga."

The voice that answered was slightly hoarse but calm and confident. Nugyen detected no fear or apprehension in the tone.

"Who's there?"

"I am Colonel Nguyen of the Army of the Socialist Republic of Vietnam. I am informed by my commanding officer that you wish to speak with a representative of the army. I am listening."

"Tell the manager to let you in with his passkey — slowly and carefully. I am armed."

Nguyen nodded to the manager, who fumbled with his keys while the other staff members scrambled in both directions, clear of the door. As he slowly pushed the door open, Nguyen saw the American propped up in the bed across the room, the pistol resting on a pillow in his lap with the muzzle commanding the door. He entered slowly, his hands held high and his head slightly bowed. The door closed automatically behind him as the manager released it.

"Turn around for me, please, Colonel."

Nguyen complied. He was wearing only the short-sleeved, green summer uniform of the army, and the American, satisfied that he concealed no weapons, motioned for him to sit in a straight-back chair against the opposite wall.

The two sat in silence sizing each other up for a brief time, less than a minute, but it seemed forever to Nguyen, time being somewhat distorted as it is at the deadly end of a gun barrel. Finally the American laid his weapon down on the pillow and spoke in an accent he had heard before. This American was a southerner.

"Would you be so kind as to hand me a bottle of water out of the minibar over there, please, sir?"

Nguyen took the two steps to the small refrigerator, then slowly and carefully crossed to the foot of the bed and offered the bottle to the American. The hand that took the water from him trembled slightly, like the lone, last leaf at the end of a painfully thin, dry branch of an arm. He struggled with the cap for a moment.

"May I?" offered Nguyen.

The American gratefully handed the bottle back, supporting one frail arm with the other. Nguyen twisted off the cap in one fluid motion he had taken for granted until now and then handed it back to the American, who reached for a medicine bottle on the nightstand. With some effort he opened the bottle on his own and dumped a small purple tablet into the palm of his hand.

Nguyen didn't need a doctor to tell him that this American was gravely ill. He had seen the ravages of cancer before. Several forms of the disease were rampant in Cu Chi. Some said the great clouds of chemicals that the Americans dumped on Vietnam and Cambodia during the war had caused it. There were rumors that some American veterans became ill years after their service, and that the government in the United States had been forced to pay settlements to some veterans' families. The official Vietnamese government line was that there were no lasting effects from Agent Orange or the other substances that the Americans had used to defoliate the countryside, denying the Communist guerrillas cover and food. After all, Vietnam was a nation that depended on agriculture and in the years since the war had become one of the world's leading exporters of rice. It was better to take care of her own and not risk the damage that continued talk of ground water contamination could do to the already shaky economy. Nearly all the affected Vietnamese were dead now anyway, joining a million of their countrymen as casualties of the war.

"Are you in pain?"

The American forced a smile. "You could say that. You know, it ain't the pain that bothers me. It's the weakness — "

The American stopped, suddenly realizing that the colonel had sussed him out. It didn't surprise him that much. He judged Nguyen's age to be near his own so he was obviously a veteran, and the American had developed a profound respect for his enemy during the war. The Vietnamese seemed to have an uncanny ability to predict what the U.S. troops were going to do before they did it, and more important, they possessed the will to act decisively.

"— the uh-h-h — weakness in my legs. The morphine still helps the pain some, but it can't get me up out of this damn bed. See, there's the problem, Colonel. The management of this establishment seems to be concerned about my ability to pay my bill, as well they should 'cause I'm flat broke. When I checked into this lovely establishment two weeks ago, I paid my room up through day before yesterday. You see, Colonel, it was never my intention to deceive anybody. I simply didn't believe that I would live this long."

The American searched Nguyen's face for a reaction. *I'd sure hate to play poker with this sonofabitch.* The colonel only listened and watched as if studying a puzzle. Hoping to force the issue, the American decided to play his hole card.

"Actually, Colonel, I intend to die right here in this bed."

No surprise. No judgment. Merely gathering information before embarking on a plan of action.

"Well, that is, I did. Sometimes things just don't work out the way we plan them. The doctor in Amsterdam gave me six months — nine tops. So I decided that I had just enough time left to see a few places I haven't been. The initial list was too long to be practical so I had to make some tough calls. In the end I narrowed it down to a pretty hokey itinerary — the Acropolis in Athens, all the usual Jesus things in Jerusalem, Marrakech — that was pretty cool — the pyramids in Egypt, various Buddhist shrines, the Taj Mahal in India, and Angkor Wat in Cambodia. I mean I've always specialized in sort of . . . out-of-the-way places, so I missed a lot of the tourist spots."

He suddenly realized that he had been rattling on, his tongue lubricated by the latest dose of morphine announcing its arrival in his cerebral cortex. The colonel only sat there as stoic as any limestone Buddha, watching and listening.

"No offense, Colonel, but do you have any fucking idea what I'm saying to you?"

The slightest hint of a smile encroached on Nguyen's face, a barely perceptible spasm at the corner of the mouth, a faint flash from within opaque black eyes.

"Though my accent leaves a lot to be desired and my vocabulary of American slang is somewhat archaic, I understand English perfectly, Mr. Engle. So Vietnam was on this list of yours?"

"Oh, hell no, Colonel. This here is my old stompin' grounds — '67 and '68 — I flew observation planes for the army — O-2's. You might say I learned my trade here. As much as I hated that war, I always wondered what this country would be like in peacetime. It really is a beautiful place. Truth is, I spent some of the best days and nights of my life right here in this hotel — especially the nights. Now, here I am about to shed this mortal coil and I got no wife, no kids. Hell, I haven't even answered to my own name in ten years. I lost a friend or two here during the war; good friends, good men, so this just seemed like as good a place as any to die."

Inwardly the colonel's mind was reeling. *Die, here? In the Caravelle?* Not exactly what the Party had in mind when they initiated the new policy of "openness." He tried to choose his words carefully, to maintain the placidity that had gotten him this far. This man was dying, drugged, desperate, and probably dangerous. He was searching the haggard face for a sign, any subtle suggestion as to how to proceed when the monologue ended abruptly and the American engaged him directly.

"How old are you, Colonel Nguyen, if you don't mind me asking?"

"Not at all. I will be forty-nine on my next birthday."

"I'll be damned. I'm forty-nine now. So you fought in the war?"

"Yes."

"And during the war how many Americans did you kill? Yourself, by your own hand?"

Nugyen's poker face was beginning to dissolve.

"I don't know . . . uh, it was wartime . . . there were no faces. They were just the enemy. Surely you — "

"No, Colonel, I was an O-2 pilot. I just flew around in my little unarmed plane and enjoyed the scenery. When a unit in the field called in an artillery strike, I spotted the smoke and let the boys back on the battery know how they were doin' — 'You're gettin' warm! Nope, you're gettin' cold again' — then I turned around and headed for home and had a cold beer or two before I went to bed — that is, until the intelligence boys spotted me and had me reassigned. Don't get me wrong now.

I've got plenty of blood on my conscience, if not on my hands. I was just on the side with all the technology. C'mon, Colonel. Let's talk body count. How many? Ten? Twenty?"

Nguyen had regained his composure somewhat, so his answer came back cold and flat.

"More."

"So Colonel, I ask you, to a man like you, a soldier — a man who has taken more than twenty lives with his own hands — in the line of duty, mind you — what's one dead American, more or less?"

Nguyen stood on the sidewalk in front of the Caravelle for a while and smoked and watched the endless procession of motorbikes circling Lam Son Square, most carrying a passenger; a young girl dressed in her weekend best riding sidesaddle behind her suitor. It was like this every Saturday night, the Vietnamese version of cruising Hollywood Boulevard. Saigon, the center of the metropolitan area renamed Ho Chi Minh City at the end of the war, had been the seat of the American occupation. Until the army sent him to the university in Hanoi to study languages, Nguyen had never realized how deeply the Americans had imprinted the South. They had managed in ten short years, a blink of an eye in Vietnamese history, to all but wipe out the French colonial gentility left behind by their predecessors. There was nothing like Lam Son Square in Hanoi. The blazing neon and constant rattle of small engines were derivatively American and patently Saigonese.

Nguyen let his cigarette fall to the pavement and crushed it out with the toe of his highly polished shoe. He crossed the street in the middle of the block, paying no attention to the traffic, instinctively never varying his pace and trusting the motorbikes and cyclos to miss him in Vietnamese fashion. In New

York he would surely have been struck by a taxi or a bus and killed, as he was completely oblivious to his surroundings. His eyes were still blinded by the steady stare of the emaciated American in Room 817 in the Caravelle Hotel. Strange words from dry, cracked lips echoed eerily in his ears.

What's one dead American, more or less?

The meaning of the words had become clear to him slowly, like a message inscribed in invisible ink held to a flickering candle: *This American is asking me to take his life. Why me? He has the gun. Why doesn't he just do it himself?*

Nguyen reached the other side of the street, entering a dark doorway and climbing a flight of stairs to a small café that overlooked the busy square. He ordered Vietnamese coffee, strong and sweet, made with sweetened condensed milk. When he picked up his spoon to stir the mixture, he noticed that his hand was shaking.

When Nguyen left the Caravelle, he had told the nervous hotel manager that he had to consult his superiors before taking any action to deal with the unwanted guest in 817, which was a lie. The Army of the Socialist Republic of Vietnam didn't work like that. When Nguyen had left General Cao's office that afternoon, he had accepted the responsibility of dealing with the American. Not that he had any choice — a soldier simply accepts an order from a superior officer and carries it out without question. General Cao had fulfilled his responsibility to his superiors when he selected Nugyen for the duty and now his part was done. He expected Nguyen to return to his office and report that the problem had been resolved. He wouldn't be particularly interested in the details beyond satisfying himself that the job was done. And Nguyen expected no less of himself.

Not that he was even considering doing as the American asked. He was a soldier, not an executioner, and he had seen enough blood to last a lifetime. Since the end of the war he had been a translator, working with foreign officers and businessmen. He had hoped that his days of dealing with life-and-death situations were behind him. Well, no matter — an order is an order. His was only to find a way to defuse the situation, quickly and quietly. But how? The man was obviously unstable and he was armed. It was just a matter of time before the police presence in the hotel attracted the attention of a journalist or a television reporter.

As the night wore on and the waiter brought coffee after coffee, each accompanied by at least two cigarettes, quiet, icy resolve began to slowly descend on Nguyen like an early morning jungle mist, as panic was simply not an option.

It reminded him of the aftermath of his first encounter with an American "tunnel rat" six feet beneath the bomb- and chemical-ravaged landscape of Cu Chi during the war. He had lain perfectly still in the stifling heat and oppressive darkness for over an hour, cut off from his planned escape route by one of the huge dogs that the Americans trained to ferret out human prey in the endless maze of tunnels that crisscrossed the district. When the big German shepherd found him, he had strangled it with his bare hands, the poor beast's great bulk hampering its movement in the narrow crawlspace, but not before it had inflicted a nasty bite on Nguyen's forearm. The same fate awaited the shepherd's master as he telegraphed his presence by leading with his flashlight and his pistol before peering down into the passage. Nguyen grabbed him by both wrists, simultaneously disarming and blinding him as he pulled the man down into the darkness. The flashlight landed near the erstwhile intruder's head, spilling just enough canned yellow light across the earthen floor that Nguyen was forced to watch in horror as death fixed the pale, youthful face into an almost comical mask of wide-eyed surprise. It was the face that Nguyen would attach to every soul he dispatched to the next world for the rest of the war.

But now there was a new face, not so different from his own, once the veneer of race and culture was stripped away. The face of a soldier who, like himself, had lived through a horror that would define him for the remainder of his life. This man was no coward. He was simply unable to take even one more human life, including his own. Now this former adversary had returned to the crucible of his worst nightmares to die. Maybe he believed that by repatriating his demons he could rest, and the war, for him, would finally be over.

Nguyen sat in the café all night, watching as the motorized procession circling the square below dwindled down to the odd cyclo. Occasionally he glanced up at the Caravelle, and each time another window had gone dark, as its anonymous occupant retired for the night, until a lone rectangular beacon shined from a single room on the eighth floor. He watched the neon fading, its contrasting medium slowly but surely compromised by the encroaching sun. Around 7:30 or 8:00, with the new day in full swing, he paid his bill and steeled himself to run the gauntlet, once again, back across the square, threading his way between the lines of speeding motorbikes and tenacious cyclos to the Caravelle Hotel. He knew what he must do.

"You look like hell, Colonel Nguyen."

"I did not sleep well, Mr. Engle. And how are you feeling today?"

Nguyen regretted his choice of words, intended as merely

one of his repertoire of standard American greetings, as soon as he had opened his mouth. The American got the wrong idea, just as Nguyen had feared, but his reaction was surprising. He laughed out loud — a great American belly laugh.

"No such luck, Colonel. As a matter of fact I'm feeling pretty damn good today. You know that morphine is a god-damn miracle drug. I feel like a million bucks —" A grimace and a sharp shallow breath gave him away. "Well, a thousand anyway. You were hopin' I'd just give out during the night, weren't you? Well, so was I, Colonel, so was I."

"My apologies, Mr. Engle, my choice of words was unfortu-nate. I only meant to inquire after your well-being and I am happy to see you are feeling better today."

"Don't worry about it, Colonel. Have you given any thought to my request?"

"I assumed that you were not serious, Mr. Engle. Surely you realize that as an officer in the Army of the Socialist Republic of Vietnam I am sworn to uphold the law. Euthanasia is illegal in this country, as it is in your own. I hoped that I might per-suade you to lay down your weapon and allow us to transfer you to a hospital where you can receive the medical treatment that you require."

"That's just not going to happen, Colonel. Not in this life-time." He chuckled at his own unintentional joke. "I've spent most of my life one step ahead of the law, Colonel, and in all that time I've never spent a single, solitary night behind bars. I haven't come this far to die in custody. So the way I see it, you have two options. One is to have your men come and get this pistol. Of course, I'll take a couple of 'em along with me, not to mention make a hell of a lot of noise. Or you can do it your-self, quietly and quickly, and no one will ever know."

"I cannot — will not — do that, Mr. Engle."

"Oh, you'll do it. You'll do it because it's the only way out of a potentially embarrassing situation. A situation that, evidently, has become your responsibility. Yeah, you'll do it all right, Colonel, it's just a matter of time. And if you think you can just sit and wait until I fall asleep, think again."

There was a second pill bottle on the nightstand. Nguyen had noticed it — he noticed everything — but he had assumed it contained another prescription from Amsterdam. The American picked it up, holding it up between a skeletal thumb and forefinger so that Nguyen could see that it was almost full of small white tablets.

"You can't get this stuff in the States anymore, Colonel, but methamphetamine is still easy to come by in Vietnam. Very civilized of you folks, I think. Eventually you will be forced to do as I ask. Meanwhile, have a seat. Would you like a drink? Smoke?"

Nguyen started to speak — and then he stopped. He accepted the offered Marlboro, looked around and located the straight-backed wooden chair, and, pulling it around to the American's bedside, he sat down and lit up. The American mistakenly perceived the change in demeanor as surrender or at least resignation.

"Is there anything I can get for you, Mr. Engle? Water, perhaps?"

"Yeah, it's about time for my mornin' fix."

He fumbled for the bottles on the nightstand, taking a pill from each bottle and washing them down with a swallow of water from the plastic bottle that Nguyen again opened for him. Nguyen noticed that there were only two or three morphine tablets remaining.

"What do you intend to do when the morphine is finished, Mr. Engle?"

"Well, I don't know, Colonel." He picked up the bottle again, regarding it with obvious amusement. "I figured I'd give out before the pills would. There were two hundred one-grain tablets in this bottle when I left Amsterdam. Of course, I didn't need 'em every day like I do now. Oh yeah, I'm sure I've got one hell of a habit goin' all right, but what the fuck. Still I only take 'em when I really hurt. Thing is, here lately I really hurt most of the time."

Nguyen pointed to the phone by the bed. "May I?"

The American reverted back to poker psychology, his eyes scanning up and down Nguyen's body searching in vain for a "tell," but, as expected, found nothing. "Go ahead."

Nguyen picked up the phone and dialed. When someone on the other end answered, obviously a subordinate, Nguyen spoke briefly in clipped, curt Vietnamese and then hung up.

"You said you were an O-2 pilot, Mr. Engle. Where were you stationed?"

"Cu Chi Army Base."

"And your tour of duty?"

"November '67 to December '68."

Cu Chi — '67–'68. The fetid atmosphere in the tunnels. The profound darkness in the deep passageways as he and his comrades lay on their bellies during the hottest part of the day. Moving as little as possible to conserve oxygen, the guerrillas waited out the sun while above them the Americans and their South Vietnamese counterparts went about the business of an army of occupation. Occasionally individual guerrillas or small teams would venture out into the light on one mission or another. But the night belonged to the National Liberation Front, called Viet Cong by their enemies. They issued from their underground strongholds under cover of darkness, safe from the prying eyes of helicopter and O-2 pilots. Cu Chi was the one part of the South that the Americans could never "pacify." Its people were staunchly nationalist, if not pro-Communist, and they supported fighting men with food from their fields and supplies stolen or scammed from the Americans.

"You know Cu Chi, Colonel?"

"I was born in Ben Duoc."

"Get outta here! I flew over that hellhole hundreds of times. Definitely Indian country. I even had a close encounter with a rocket over Ben Duoc once. There was some crazy fucker in that area that had evidently captured himself a rocket launcher and a pretty good supply of rockets. 'Ben Duoc Ben' we called him. He shot at every O-2 that overflew the village for a solid month. Damn near got me. I was just making my turn for home and here came a fuckin' rocket. Sucker rose straight up out of a grove of trees. Couldn't have missed me by more than a few feet. Really rattled me for a minute there. I mean I was flying an unarmed aircraft. No one had ever actually shot at me before. Ol' Bobby Harper actually caught one out there one day. Tore his port boom all to hell. It's a miracle he made it back to base."

Nguyen started, his placid demeanor evaporating once and for all.

"What did you say the pilot's name was?"

"Bobby Harper. Great big fella from Arkansas."

"But he did make it safely back to base?"

"Yeah. Not the prettiest landing of the war, mind you, but any landing you walk away from is a good one."

Nguyen breathed an audible sigh. "I have often wondered."

In the same instant that the American realized that sitting before him was none other than Ben Duoc Ben, someone knocked on the door. It was a young army officer who spoke to Nguyen through the door. The colonel rose and after receiving wordless permission from the American walked to the door and opened it just enough to receive a small package from the unseen courier.

"This should help with the pain. Unfortunately, we have no morphine in tablet form in our small hospital."

The American received the package gratefully, opening it with some effort. Inside were five small vials of golden-colored liquid and a half-dozen disposable syringes. He chuckled, almost to himself as he removed one vial and one syringe, pulling the cap off of the syringe with his teeth to expose the sharp needle. As he inverted the vial and began to fill the syringe, he winked at the colonel.

"Got to be careful about this. Don't want to overdose or get an air bubble in our brain or anything like that." The task complete, the American searched around the room for something to serve as a tourniquet. "Colonel, if you'd be so kind as to hand me my belt over there — hanging on the bathroom door."

Nguyen looked back over his shoulder and located the belt, rose, and crossed the room in two or three steps. When he returned he sat on the edge of the bed and gently, almost tenderly wrapped the belt around the top of the American's wasted arm without being asked, looping it through the buckle to form a noose. As he tightened the belt the veins in the American's arm stood at attention to receive the needle and its straw-colored cargo, both remedy and poison, mercy and death. He found his mark effortlessly, and as Nguyen released the belt the American eased back into his pillows and closed his eyes. The relief on his face radiated out into the room so that even Nguyen sighed audibly when the morphine took effect.

The American regarded Nguyen through half-opened eyes.

"You know, Colonel, it's ironic. I flew tons of morphine-base out of Laos and Burma during the war. I believed the CIA boys when they told me that no American would be hurt, and what's worse, I believed that as long as only the enemy was being poisoned then everything was OK. As long as it was those 'other people' that died. You people."

Nguyen shrugged. "The war brought with it many evils, Mr. Engle. War always does. It is true, refined heroin was unknown in Vietnam before the war, but opium has been here for centuries. The drug traffic would not have been possible without the cooperation of some of my countrymen. They were greedy, and greed is the mother of treachery. There were many traitors here in the South."

"I had you figured for a northerner — you being a colonel and all. I wasn't aware there were any high-ranking officers from the South — fortunes of war and all that."

"There are a few of us, mostly we who served in the tunnels in Cu Chi, though only a handful of us survived the war, I'm afraid. We were a guerrilla army, not career soldiers. Many went back to their callings as teachers or farmers or whatever they were doing before, only to die years later of —"

The American finished Nguyen's sentence.

"Cancer. Yeah I know. We dumped a lot of shit on that area. Horrible, poisonous shit. There were barrels and barrels of chemicals on that base. Sometimes it would come in from the states by the planeload. We never asked about what it was or if it was safe to handle. It never occurred to us that if it could kill a two-hundred-year-old banyan tree, it could kill us. Some of the guys on the ground got sick immediately. You know, nausea, headaches, and the like. Usually the symptoms went away in a few days and no one made the connection. Then they got home. There was even a little settlement from the government years later, but not without a fight. Of course I wasn't around for that. I haven't been home in more than twenty years, except for a wild-ass week in Texas a while back."

"Do you miss it?"

"Sometimes. But you get used to it after a while. To tell you the truth, it's been so long since I've been home I don't really remember what it feels like. Most of the guys I knew were surprised when they got home and were called 'baby-killer' in their own hometowns, but not me. I knew better. I guess I'd just seen too much. Three weeks after I got home, I flew my first load of pot out of Michoacán for a friend of mine in San Diego. I never looked back. It was easier that way. I just kept movin', whichever way the wind blew. Just fly. Any cargo. Anywhere. Anytime. Somewhere along the road I lost my name, my past, my country — maybe even my soul — but I don't really have any regrets. My luck finally ran out over Mexico a few years back, and I even survived that, though I had to kind of retire. Since then I've just drifted around Europe and Asia, drawing money from accounts I had rat-holed away in Switzerland and the Caymans. Then about a year ago I got to feeling poorly in Amsterdam and, well, here we are."

The American went on for hours, retracing his travels from Amsterdam across Europe and the Mideast to the Asian subcontinent. Nguyen sat and listened intently, genuinely enthralled by the American's tales of exotic places. Nguyen had never been outside of Vietnam. Travel abroad was forbidden for years following the war. The government's new policy of "openness" in practice only opened the borders in one direction, except for travel on official business. In any case leaving the country that he had fought so fiercely to liberate had simply never occurred to Nguyen. Periodically he interrupted

the American with questions, and the American answered the
ones that he could, bringing color and substance to the one-di-
mensional written accounts of life in the outside world offered
by the state-operated newspapers. When it became obvious to
Nguyen that the American was in pain, he helped him inject
another dose of morphine and then a few hours later another.
Every dose was followed by another hit of speed, and the
American's mouth became dry and his lips were sore and
cracked. Around six in the evening of the second day, Nguyen
sent for a case of bottled water and more morphine, which was
promptly delivered.

Over most of the third day, Nguyen told the American about
the hard years after the war, when Vietnam was cut off from
most of the world as she struggled to rebuild. He told of the
flood of former cadres from the North — the *can bo* — filling
all of the newly created government posts. Hundreds of thousands of southerners were sent to reeducation camps, including some that had fought for the cause, but Nguyen was lucky.
His service and loyalty to the Party was never questioned,
and his superiors recognized his skill with languages. He traveled north to study at the university in Hanoi, and when he
returned he went to work at the army's Information Office,
where his progress was sure if not quite as fast as his northern coworkers. The American remarked that conditions in
postreunification Vietnam were similar to the period following
the American Civil War, when northern carpetbaggers poured
into the southern states to exploit the "Reconstruction" of the
former Confederacy. This prompted a flood of questions from
Nguyen, who was completely ignorant of American history
and unaware that there had ever been a civil war in the States.
He was even more surprised that his Great Enemy across the
water had a colonial past and was born of revolution.

"Well, Colonel, it wasn't that kind of revolution. Not a people's revolution, anyway. It was more of a gentleman's insurrection, conceived by wealthy farmers who were tired of sending the fruits of their labor — in some cases slave labor — back to England. I don't think you could really call them revolutionaries in socialist terms."

For five days and nights Nguyen sat at the American's bedside, rising only to go to the bathroom or to receive food, water, and morphine through a crack in the door. He catnapped periodically, sitting straight up in the chair and resting his head against the wall behind him. His men were right outside the door and the American wasn't going anywhere anyway. By the morning of the fourth day the American was too weak to get out of bed, and Nguyen sent for a bedpan, which he helped the dying man use when he needed to. Somewhere along the line both had forgotten all about the pistol, even though it lay in plain sight on the bed. Also forgotten were the amphetamine tablets on the nightstand. There was no need for the American to stay awake anymore, as a kind of bond was forged between them, a wordless trust wrought in the fire of their differences and quenched in their limited common experience. The differences were overwhelming. The American was a talker, like every American that Nguyen had met. Nguyen, however, was culturally predisposed, politically indoctrinated, as well as militarily trained to listen. Originally he was listening and watching for an opportunity to disarm the American and diffuse "this dangerous situation," per his orders, but that didn't concern him anymore. He knew he had only to be patient, and time and cancer would produce a result satisfactory to his superiors and at the same time discharge this newfound responsibility to the American. After all, the American only wanted to die in peace. Had he seen a clear conflict between the American's dying wish and his own duty to his country, things would be completely different. He was first and foremost a patriot, another difference between him and the American.

"How does one face the horror and deprivation of war without fervor?"

"I was drafted. Don't get me wrong. I believed everything I was taught in school, all that 'defenders of the free world' crap when I went in. I was actually pretty gung ho when I arrived in-country. History told me that the U.S. Army had never been defeated and I had no reason to believe that the outcome of this little war would be any different. Hell, I had a pretty good deal. O-2 pilots are enlisted men with wings. A staff sergeant on the ground is humpin' along in the bush with the grunts with a better-than-average chance of getting his ass shot off or stepping on something that explodes or worse. I figured I'd do my bit and go back to the States and the next shift would mop up. Then I transferred to Intelligence, thinking that was going to be an even sweeter deal, and I started seeing things that I didn't understand. Shadowy, sickening stuff that I knew wasn't OK. As far as the invincibility thing goes, Tet pretty much took care of that."

The look on Nguyen's face told the American that another question was forthcoming.

"Where were you the night that the Tet Offensive began, Mr. Engle?"

"I was here, Colonel. Right here in Room 817 in the Caravelle Hotel."

In the first hours of January 21, 1968, seventy thousand Vietnamese troops, mostly guerrillas, simultaneously attacked every urban center under American control. The Americans were caught off guard, having committed large numbers of troops and air power to rescuing a company of Marines besieged for more than a week at Khe Sanh, near the border with Laos. The entire Khe Sanh operation was a ploy designed to siphon defenses away from more than one hundred other targets all over Vietnam. Violating the cease-fire traditionally observed for Tet, the Chinese lunar New Year, the guerrillas struck in concert, killing two thousand Americans and twice as many South Vietnamese soldiers. Their own losses were much greater, totaling over twenty thousand, and the offensive failed in its objective of sparking a popular revolt in the South. But the most significant casualty of the Tet Offensive was the American people's willingness to support the war in Vietnam. While Americans at home watched on television, National Liberation Front guerrillas, called Viet Cong by the Americans, infiltrated and held parts of the American Embassy for more than six hours. Neither the brave young men who died attacking the embassy nor their comrades who were fighting and dying around the country ever knew that the war, for all practical purposes, had been won that night. Including Nguyen.

"The entire Saigon operation was staged from the tunnel system in Cu Chi. My unit left the tunnels around midnight and traveled over ten miles through the bush in what would have been total darkness for anyone who had not spent months living and training several meters below the ground. Our eyes were so sensitive to light that we moved quickly and surely, as if it were daylight. We attacked the army base at Cu Chi with mortars and RPGs (rocket-propelled grenades). Of the thirty men in my unit only three of us survived until the morning when, out of ammunition and blinded by the rising sun, we withdrew to the tunnels. We had not even penetrated the outer defenses of the base. And the worst was yet to come. The American Air Force rained death down on Cu Chi district for a solid month, and then ground troops moved in to finish the job. When it was all over, the National Liberation Front had, for all practical purposes, ceased to exist. The fields I had played and worked in as a boy were laid waste and would not bear crops for another ten years. Even the air was unfit to breathe. We did manage to hit a large ammunition dump. It was a lucky shot but it was glorious. As we dragged ourselves back to our bunker, we looked over our shoulders from time to time and watched the smoke. It could be seen for miles."

"And heard." The American struggled to sit up. Nguyen helped him prop himself up with a couple of pillows. "I was up in the roof garden bar here in the Caravelle until about eleven. It was a going-away party for my girlfriend — or sort of girlfriend anyway. I excused myself and pretended to go back to the base, taking the elevator to the lobby and then, when I was reasonably sure no one was watchin', I slipped back up the stairs to the eighth floor. Emily was an officer, an army nurse, and fraternization was strictly against regulations. We made love — badly — we were both pretty drunk and then fell asleep in each other's arms. We woke around three-thirty to a loud boom that shook downtown Saigon and lit up a good part of the northwestern sky. That was probably your ammo dump, Colonel. I threw on my clothes and left the way I came — by the stairs. I spent the rest of the night trying to get back to the base but there was no fuckin' way. The city was in chaos. The rattle of small-arms fire and the rumble of armored personnel carriers loaded with GI and ARVN troops filled the night. People were runnin' around like the proverbial headless chickens — hell, you could taste the fear in the air. Suddenly our safe little American Sin City had become Indian Country."

Nguyen was literally on the edge of his chair.

"And then?"

"And then . . . I died."

It was an old joke. A shaggy dog tale in which a braggart, holding forth in his gentlemen's club, spins a yarn about his exploits in "the Great War." The American had delivered it as deadpan and straight as a Methodist minister. For an exaggerated instant Nguyen sat and stared blankly back at the American. Then, as he reconciled the literal translation, the humor sank in and he laughed out loud and long, and the American laughed with him. Nguyen tried in vain to compose himself but the hysteria was infectious, like hiccups or a catchy tune you can't get out of your head. For nearly half an hour, each time the American tried to continue with his tale he would no sooner make eye contact than Nguyen exploded into laughter again. Finally they were both giggling uncontrollably like schoolgirls, repeating the punch line over and over in between howling. Both warriors battled in vain for control, normally a long suit, but the tide could not be stemmed. It rolled over them again and again, in great orgasmic cleansing waves, retreating only when every hateful scar or stain of war had been washed away in a torrent of healing mirth. Finally exhausted, the American managed to catch his breath and offered Nguyen a straight answer to his question.

"I finally gave up and holed up in one of the whorehouses on Tu Do until daylight. It was another two days before I reached the base and reported in. I never saw or heard from Captain Emily Allison again. And you, Colonel?"

Nguyen was still mopping away tears with a handkerchief. He managed, finally, to compose himself.

"A few of us managed to escape to the North through Cambodia. We were welcomed as heroes of the revolution. I spent the rest of the war there analyzing intercepted radio transmissions. By the time the Americans finally withdrew and the southern government collapsed, I had no family left alive in the South so I remained in Hanoi and enlisted in the Regular Army. I attended the university for two years, and when I returned I was assigned to the Information Office in Ho Chi Minh City. I worked my way up through the ranks. I met a girl. We were married. We were blessed with two fine sons and a beautiful daughter. And then . . . I died."

Nguyen literally collapsed on the floor in front of his chair, laughing so hard that it actually hurt and pounding the floor with his fists. The American was laughing as well but the joy caught in his throat like a fishbone and shattered into a fit of coughing — sharp hacking dry heaves — that seemed to emanate from deep within his cancer-wracked body. He feared he would never catch his breath again, but suddenly Nguyen was there holding him and helping him to lean forward and expectorate into a wastepaper basket and then massaging his back until the spasm slowly subsided. When Nguyen gently lowered his head onto the pillow, the American tried to thank him but could manage no sound so he closed his eyes and fell into a deep, peaceful sleep. Sometime before sunrise on the morning of the sixth day, he died.

Nguyen had just awakened from a nap and, having been on intimate terms with death for nearly all of his life, he knew with a glance that the American was gone. To make certain he searched the tiny wrists and the pale, thin neck for a pulse and found none. He picked up the pistol from the bed, removed the clip and cleared the round in the chamber, and then, leaning over the body, picked up the phone and dialed.

"General Cao, please. It's urgent. This is Colonel Nguyen."

While Nguyen waited for the general to pick up the phone, his impeccable military bearing involuntarily returned.

"General Cao, the American is dead. No, no one was hurt. It will all be in my report. Thank you, General. It is only my duty."

As he left Room 817, Nguyen turned for one final look before he allowed the soldiers to enter and remove the body. Nguyen thought that the American looked almost serene, lying there, his face bathed in the first rays of the sunlight of a new day, the sound of his laughter still suspended like dandelion seeds in the air nearby, resonating in harmony with that of a former enemy's.

THE WITNESS

THE LAST SIX MILES of the drive from the city out to the state penitentiary was a dark, lonely stretch of two-lane blacktop winding through a no man's land of second-growth timber and fallow farmland — a kind of airlock between prison and the free world. The road itself was well maintained by inmate labor, smooth and even, and the late-model Lincoln glided along as if on black ice. The driver expected no traffic coming from the penitentiary this time of night (it was just after 10:00 P.M.) and he met none. He had the road to himself.

When he reached the clear-cut area surrounding the penitentiary and stopped at the perimeter gate, he squinted against the artificial daylight created by powerful halogen lamps mounted atop tall steel towers commanding the four corners of the compound. At the guard shack the officer asked him for his I.D. and recorded his license number before directing him to the visitors' center at the rear of the compound. "Two lefts and a right. Park in the roped-off area and check in at the gatehouse."

He had passed a few demonstrators standing around in a tight knot outside the perimeter. One of them, a heavyset man in his late forties, stepped out of line and met the driver with a withering gaze and mouthed the word "murderer." Actually he probably shouted out loud, but the big Lincoln was well soundproofed, so the driver heard nothing but the drone of the motor as if from a distance and the Noise — a sort of sibilant hiss in his ears that had become his almost constant companion. His mouth was dry and filled with a vaguely metallic taste. He was reminded of the anxiety attacks he sometimes suffered in law school, but this feeling was more intense, more threatening. The light-headedness was the same, but there was no panic, no fight-or-flight response, only a profound sinking feeling and an unnatural heaviness in his arms and legs.

The protestor rejoined his colleagues on the picket line. There would be no large, loud demonstration tonight, only a handful of die-hard death penalty abolitionists. They would light their candles and hold up their signs until the prison press officer came out and announced that it was all over. Then they would pack up and head home. "See you next week." And the same ragtag group of five or six would be back six days later, because in this state, fueled by fear and oiled with the ambition of politicians, the death machine was in high gear.

The pro–death penalty groups had stopped attending executions altogether. There was no need. There would be no last-minute stay, no clemency from the governor. It had all become routine.

He parked the car and locked it, laughing nervously to himself as he realized there probably wasn't a safer place to park in the state. This was the most secure prison tax-dollars could build. The new "Supermax" facility was the governor and the attorney general's showpiece, built specifically to house the state's most dangerous inmates: the murderers, rapists, and habitual armed robbers. Just beyond that last gate was "A" Unit — death row and the Death House itself. It was highly unlikely there was an un-incarcerated criminal within a hundred miles. Especially not tonight.

His name was Gordon Elliot and he had come to this god-forsaken place to witness an execution. An eye for an eye, justice if you will. Tonight the state would set things right, and the nightmare would finally be over. At least that's what he was telling himself.

It had been nearly twelve years since Andres Camacho had been arrested for killing Joan Elliot. The local news had been dominated by the brutal crime for several months. Back then every lurid detail had been painstakingly inscribed on video-tape and replayed again and again on the evening news. In the years that followed, most of the footage had been recorded over to make room for some more recent atrocity, or something as mundane as a local high school's trip to the state basketball tournament. Oh, there was still a short clip of Camacho being led from the courtroom in manacles archived somewhere in the vault, and tomorrow when he was dead they would haul it out and air about fifteen seconds of it on *The Morning Show*, but no one would pay any attention. Twelve years had gone by now, and no one was really interested in the story of a forty-six-year-old travel agent, brutally raped and strangled in her home. They had all but forgotten about the gardener, an illegal alien from El Salvador, who was arrested as he tried to make a run for the Mexican border in Joan Elliot's Jeep Cherokee. And no one remembered her husband, Gordon, the successful corporate attorney, crying like a baby on the ten o'clock news.

Executions themselves had become far too commonplace to be front-page news in any medium. This one would be a postscript *after* the weather and *after* the sports, and then, only in the city where the murder had occurred.

"This way, Mr. Elliot." The assistant warden, Allen Earnhardt, greeted him at the gatehouse and waited while he signed in and was frisked. Gordon followed the little man, a full foot shorter than his six feet five, through the double glass doors of the visitors' center and through what seemed like miles of green-and-white-tiled hallway. Finally he was ushered into a bare-bones kind of a lounge, normally used by prison employees for coffee breaks. One step further, he thought to himself, and he would have passed out cold on the floor.

The harsh fluorescent lighting reflecting off the freshly painted off-white surfaces cast a surreal pall over the room. Inside there was a Coke machine, some uncomfortable-looking institutional furniture, and for this occasion one of those long, heavy-duty Formica-top folding tables covered in a red-and-white-checked tablecloth. On the table were two large coffee urns (regular and decaf), an assortment of store-bought cookies, and a plate of pimento cheese sandwiches with the crusts cut off. The coffee was going fast, but no one except the wire service reporter was eating anything.

Russell McBride was leaning against the Coke machine with a cup of coffee in one hand, talking to a couple of the guards, with a mouthful of pimento cheese when he spotted Gordon. Assistant Warden Earnhardt grabbed Gordon's coat sleeve at the elbow and tugged him along in a vain attempt to avoid the large reporter who simply imposed his substantial girth in their path.

"Mr. Elliot, I'm Russ McBride from A.P. How you doin', counselor?"

The reporter offered an overly firm handshake and an inappropriate grin. His voice seemed to originate from a great distance, though his large round face was only inches away. Gordon for some reason became fixated on his hair. It was one of those painfully obvious comb-over jobs, the kind that makes you wonder why he even bothered. It was parted just above his left ear and stretched so tautly across his enormous head that the tension was palpable. McBride continued talking, but that Noise was still there, like angry hornets between Gordon's ears. One phrase stood out over the din: "It's always tough the first time."

Gordon was speechless but his face must have betrayed his shock. *The first time?*

"Oh, yeah, this is my sixty-fourth execution," McBride stated, proudly. "Don't worry, these boys have it down to a science. It'll all be over before you know it and you can get on with your life."

Gordon was secretly impressed.

Earnhardt, temporarily paralyzed by McBride's aggressive approach, suddenly sputtered back to life.

"Now, Russ, you know the rules." He quickly shepherded Gordon across the room to an ugly, green Naugahyde chair. "Can I get you something, Mr. Elliot? A cup of coffee maybe?"

"No, thank you." The words came out hoarse and dry as if he was speaking for the first time in years. He plopped down in the ugly chair, hoping the assistant warden didn't notice that his knees gave out at the last second.

"All right, then. You just wait right here and Warden Larkin will be along to talk to you directly."

Earnhardt stopped to talk to McBride before leaving the room. Although the conversation took place out of Gordon's earshot, the participants were animated enough that it was obvious that Earnhardt was admonishing McBride for his breach of protocol, and that McBride for his part couldn't care less. Standing next to McBride, looking more than a little embarrassed for her chosen profession, was the reporter from the local newspaper, a young woman in her mid-twenties.

Of all the people in the room, Lorrie White looked the most out of place. Outwardly she was the kind of girl you saw all over this town of twenty thousand. It was easier to imagine her editing a social column or even better, accenting long-stemmed roses with baby's breath at the local florist. Just a little job to keep her busy until the right man came along. One of the wardens at the prison perhaps? Certainly either scenario was a lot closer to what her parents had in mind when they sent her off to college. When she came home with a degree in journalism and applied at the *Dispatch*, "A" Unit was just hitting its stride. Her editor was dubious when she asked to be assigned to the first execution of a woman in the state. The truth of the matter was, he didn't have anyone on staff who was interested in covering the Death House. That was a year and seventeen killings ago, and now the Death House was Lorrie White's undisputed beat.

Gordon looked around the room. Besides the two reporters there were a handful of correctional officers and state police standing around. Occasionally one of them would look Gordon's way, but other than that there was no attempt to make any other sort of contact. The cops stayed on their side of the room and Gordon on his, and everyone seemed perfectly comfortable with that. From time to time other prison officials, "suits" like Earnhardt, would enter the room and fix themselves a cup of coffee, and after exchanging barely audible acknowledgments with their coworkers, go on about their business. It was somehow clear that everyone here had a task to perform, their own fraction of a larger protocol carefully thought out by their superiors.

They had spent the morning rehearsing a procedure that they all knew by heart. Since capital punishment was resumed in 1977, the state had carried out, in this very prison, 159 neat, clinical executions by lethal injection. Well, in the beginning there had actually been a few problems.

A good many of the inmates who died in "A" Unit had been lifelong drug addicts, and when the time had come to insert the IV lines, their needle-ravaged veins, lurking beneath a bunker of scar tissue, often eluded the technicians. For such cases an alternative procedure where the needle was inserted into less-trafficked veins in the groin area was adopted. Sometimes, in those early days, the dosage of the deadly mixture of drugs that flowed through the tubes was poorly calculated, and the inmate died slowly, gasping for breath. Some experienced violent convulsions, and one inmate, contorting in the throes of death, even managed to turn the gurney over, prompting the state to design and install a permanent gurney, bolted securely to the concrete floor. In the official press releases from the prison the incidents were termed "unfortunate." Behind closed doors in the administration building, however, every botched execution was taken very seriously. This sort of incident defeated the very purpose of the lethal injection method, which was, after all, intended to spare the executioners and the witnesses any macabre spectacle. Each time there was a "glitch," the warden would call a meeting and a new procedure, specifically formulated to correct the current problem, would be introduced into the protocol. Over time the warden and his men slowly but surely worked the bugs out. In the past fifteen years, through determination and practice, they had achieved an eerie level of efficiency, and the procedure had become nearly flawless.

And a flawless procedure was exactly what Gordon Elliot wanted. More than anyone else present, with the possible exception of Andres Camacho, Gordon needed this thing to go quickly and smoothly.

The door opened and Assistant Warden Earnhardt emerged with Lieutenant Roscoe Abraham and another man whom Gordon didn't recognize in tow. Lieutenant Abraham was the one cop in the room that Gordon was glad to see. He took some sort of comfort in the detective's presence. After all, Abraham was the lead investigator on his wife's case and at least he was a familiar face. He was tall and well built for a man in his early sixties. His hair and beard were shot through with that combination of snow white and iron gray that black men display when they've reached venerability. His voice was low and resonant and his manner gentle, if a little patronizing, like a grandfather talking to a small child. Gordon had always found it reassuring. Abraham had been the first policeman to interview him on the night of the murder. He had always been kind and considerate, calling Gordon everyday to inquire about how he was holding up, even picking him up in his own car and driving him down to headquarters to identify Camacho when he was captured and brought back to the city a week later. Gordon was also grateful that Abraham had never, as far as he knew, suspected him of murdering his wife. One of Gordon's law school buddies who had gone on to a successful criminal practice told him, "The husband is always the first one they go after. When they rule him out, then and only then do they start looking elsewhere." Nevertheless, Gordon had declined his friend's offer to represent him during his dealings with the police. "Why do I need a lawyer?" he asked incredulously. "I'm not a suspect." And he was right. At no time in the investigation was he a "serious" suspect in the eyes of the police.

Lieutenant Abraham leaned over Gordon, simultaneously taking his outstretched right hand firmly in his own and patting it, reassuringly, with the left.

"Gordon, this is District Attorney Adam Boquist."

Gordon knew the man looked familiar. He'd only seen Boquist on the front page of the paper before now. He was much smaller than he looked in his pictures, almost diminutive. He wore a meticulously tailored dark gray three-piece suit, and his dark hair was neatly parted and sprayed in place. He had the perfect politician's handshake, not too limp, not too firm, and he spoke in pleasant, measured, media-friendly tones. The Noise still made it extremely difficult for Gordon to make out any of the words, however. Rather he focused, once again, on unimportant details such as the watch the prosecutor wore. It was a TAG Heuer, identical to his own. He noticed it when Boquist shook his hand, along with the fact that he was left-handed. It did strike Gordon as rather odd that the DA himself was present.

Adam Boquist was the third district attorney to oversee *State vs. Camacho,* and in all of the years since Joan's murder, Gordon had never met any of them. The case was originally tried by an assistant DA named Bobby Easly, who left the prosecutors' office years ago to run for a vacant circuit judge's seat, which he won. Throughout the long appeals process Gordon had been forced to get used to a new team of prosecutors at every stage. All of them asked more or less the same questions, but some were easier to work with than others. It was never necessary for Gordon to testify again because there was no new evidence, and Camacho's appeals were strictly routine. Nevertheless, the prosecutors always wanted the victim's family present in capital cases for "the emotional factor." All that was expected of Gordon was that he suit up, show up, and look like a victim. The truth be told, that's exactly what Adam Boquist was doing in "A" Unit that night. Suiting up and showing up. After all, it was an election year.

With all of the "victim's witnesses" assembled, there was nothing left to do but wait.

Down the hall in a similar room, the "offender's witnesses" waited as well.

Mary Egan, a thirty-eight-year-old schoolteacher and activist from Northampton, Massachusetts, had never met Andres Camacho face to face. Until a week before his date with the executioner, they had only communicated by mail. She spoke no Spanish, so her letters had to be translated by Camacho's bilingual cellmate. When he asked her, in a letter dated six months before, to witness his execution, she was surprised and confused. "Why me?" She finally agreed but she still had reservations, as much about her own motives for being there as anything else. Being a witness at a killing was the ultimate badge of courage in the abolition movement. It would afford her instant credibility. Maybe Andres knew that. Maybe this was a gift. Or maybe he just wanted someone present that didn't hate him. She had never given much thought to guilt or innocence. It simply didn't matter to her. She was opposed to the death penalty, period. She paced back and forth while they waited, trying to find something inside herself to calm her and get her past the anger that threatened to overwhelm her in these last minutes. She was, after all, an abolitionist. She had spent all of her adult life writing letters, stuffing envelopes, whatever she was asked to do in the name of the movement. She had stood in vigil outside nearly every state execution site in the nation, but this time she was inside, and she couldn't shake the feeling that she was somehow helping to facilitate this one.

David Price was a well-meaning but inexperienced civil attorney who had been court-appointed to represent Andres Camacho in his federal appeals process. Actually he was a pretty damn good divorce attorney with a bright future ahead of him, until one day, four years ago, when one of the senior partners in his firm summoned Price to his office. What took place there that day was the legal profession's equivalent of a powerful warlord ordering an underling to commit hara-kiri for the honor of the firm. Price had heard of such things — the state attorney general would telephone an old law school buddy and call in a favor. Capital cases could not be seen through to a satisfactory conclusion without "competent" legal representation for the defendant. It was a political imperative. There was always danger of reversal on appeal if the attorney who handled the case was obviously inept. To remedy this, the state would contact the best, most prestigious firms, who would trot out a sacrificial lamb, arm him or her with a laundry list of motions and maneuvers, prepared of course by the firm's best criminal attorneys, and send him or her out to the slaughter. Honor was satisfied and the senior partners would reap the rewards. Somewhere down the line, the brownie points earned would be redeemed for a judgeship or a spot on the ticket in a future election.

Price left the senior partner's office that day knowing full well that his career was over. The past four years had left him a complete physical and emotional wreck. He had developed a peptic ulcer. He suffered from blinding, painful migraine headaches. He began neglecting his divorce cases to a degree that his once lucrative practice had all but completely dried up. When Camacho had finally run out of time and appeals, Price had volunteered to be present at his execution, a decision that now, with the moment at hand, he deeply regretted. Among the veteran correctional officers, the smart money said David Price wasn't going to make it.

One witness wasn't waiting in the lounge with the others. As spiritual adviser, Father Esteban Ramirez was spending this last hour alone with Camacho in the Death House itself. The prison chaplain, Russell Meeks, had picked his name more or less at random from a list of bilingual Catholic clergy engaged in ministries on death row. A Franciscan friar from Los Angeles, Father Ramirez was a vigorous seventy-two-year-old with the energy of an adolescent. When he moved briskly through his rounds in the prison, everyone in the institution moved quickly aside, partly in deference to his calling and partly in awe, inspired by the sight of the tall, white-headed cleric dressed in the long brown habit of his order. The calm countenance and fierce black eyes gave him the air of a warrior-monk, a righteous defender of the faith with a Bible in his right hand and a breastplate, emblazoned with the cross, secreted beneath his habit. When prison staffers encountered Father Ramirez in a prison corridor, they were left with the distinct impression that he just might go right through them if they impeded him on his mission, for there were souls at stake and not a second to lose.

The offender's party was rounded out by two television reporters — one from the local station and one from the city where the crime was committed. When the state began allowing victims' family members to witness executions a few years back, the witness room was divided in half. Now witnesses from both sides watched the proceedings through the same unbreakable Plexiglas window, separated by a wall that had been hastily erected down the center of the already tiny room. Space considerations dictated that the press had to be divided, more or less, equally between the two cubicles. Protocol called for the two sets of witnesses to arrive at different times, escorted to and from separate waiting areas, every move carefully choreographed to ensure they never saw each other. The idea was obviously to prevent any ugly emotional confrontations. In this case, however, all the fuss was unnecessary.

There was something different about this execution. Some of the guards picked up on it. They gossiped about it in hushed tones when they were sure no one was listening, but they couldn't quite put a finger on it.

Some of it was explainable. Camacho was from El Salvador, seventeen hundred miles to the south. All of his witnesses were strangers. His relatives were far too poor to make the trip, even if the Naturalization and Immigration Service would allow it. Only his oldest brother, Nestor, had ever been to visit. Then, five years ago, the *migra* scooped Nestor Camacho up in a raid on a West Coast garment factory and shipped him back home. Gordon and Joan Elliot had never had children. Both of Joan's parents were dead. Gordon was the only witness who was actually personally involved, and no one expected any trouble out of him.

Maybe that was it. Maybe it was Gordon Elliot himself. There was none of the soul-wracking, malignant, smoldering rage usually observed in a victim's family member who came to witness an execution. Maybe over the years he had come to terms with the horrible things that had happened to his wife. Maybe he was in shock. In any case, he was outwardly a very cool customer. He walked into that witness room, sat down in that chair, and hadn't moved an inch since. He just sat there, speaking only when spoken to by the old detective or the DA, and then his replies came in quiet, clipped, monotonous blurbs. His demeanor was more cold than calm, betraying no emotion whatsoever.

Meanwhile, across the yard in a holding cell, barely fifteen steps from the hospital gurney where he would meet his maker, Andres Camacho was preparing to die.

At the time of Joan Elliot's murder, Camacho was thirty-five and had been working for the Elliots for a little less than a year. Joan's best friend, Missy Warner, had recommended him when she moved away to Boston. Her husband, a senior partner in Gordon's firm, had retired and accepted a teaching position at Harvard Law after suffering a heart attack the year before. Their kids were grown and finished with school, and the academic life seemed to offer just the antidote to the high-pressure environment of a corporate practice.

Andy, as the Warners called him, did wonderful things with flowers of all kinds, and Joan had always been envious of their garden. She begged Gordon to hire him and against his better judgment, he gave in after putting up his usual, minimal amount of resistance. Whatever made Joan happy made Gordon's life easier. Camacho soon became part of the landscape around the Elliot house, if not a member of the family, living in a small apartment above the garage. He worked hard and was rewarded with better-than-average pay for an illegal and a generous Christmas bonus so he could buy gifts and send them home to his family in El Salvador. Joan had even learned to speak a little Spanish, and Andy was patient with her accent and helped her with her grammar. He felt fortunate to have such a kind and generous employer, and the future had looked bright. Soon, much sooner than he had expected, he would have enough money saved to pay the "coyote" to smuggle his family into the country, and they would be together again.

But now he was receiving the last rites from Father Ramirez in an eight- by ten-foot prison cell a long way from home. Chaplain Meeks had come and gone, after delivering his usual patter in his best, low, even tone. Even Camacho, who couldn't understand a single word, was left with the impression that Meeks had made the very same over-rehearsed presentation many, many times before. Father Ramirez didn't even bother to translate. He just picked up where they had left off when they were interrupted.

At 11:20, Assistant Warden Earnhardt reappeared in the victim's waiting area and held the door open for Warden Sam Larkin and Chaplain Meeks. They entered the room, Larkin first, followed by Meeks and then Earnhardt, who closed the door behind them. They stepped forward almost in unison, forming a perfect little rank across the front of the room. They had everyone's attention even before Earnhardt opened his mouth.

"May I have your attention, please? Warden Larkin would like to say a few words."

The warden took one step forward and began speaking in the same low-key, measured manner that seemed to be standard issue in this institution.

"Folks, I'm Sam Larkin, the warden."

The Noise persisted and Gordon struggled to make out a word or two and then filled in the blanks as best he could.

"I know this isn't easy for anyone concerned, my staff and I included. But we have a job to do. This gentleman is Chaplain Meeks." Meeks took a half step forward, careful not to supersede his superior. "He is here for your benefit as well as the inmate's. If you have any needs of a spiritual nature, feel free to take them up with him. Now there are some rules and procedures that have to be observed for the good of all and your cooperation is appreciated. We will go over a few of these at this time."

Larkin paused and waited for Meeks to fall back into line.

"Let me remind you that we are all here to help in any way we can. If anyone should feel faint, please let us know now so the officers can keep an eye on you. We don't want anyone hurting themselves. Feeling a little funny in these circumstances is certainly nothing to be ashamed of, and our officers are trained to deal with little emergencies like that. Another thing I need to bring up is the issue of the press. There are reporters present. They are all veterans and they know the rules."

Earnhardt, standing at "parade rest" behind the Warden, shot a sidelong glance in the general direction of Russ Mc-Bride.

"They will not ask to speak to you unless you approach them yourselves. However, they are reporters, and they are present to record what they see and hear. If you make a comment to anyone during these proceedings and one of them overhears it, he or she will probably write it down. That is their job."

Suddenly Warden Larkin's entire demeanor changed.

"Now, let me tell you a little bit about what you can expect to happen here tonight."

He looked down at his watch.

"In about fifteen minutes I will make two phone calls. The first, to the state attorney general. The second, to the governor.

I will ask if there are any stays or clemency pending that would cause the suspension of these proceedings here tonight. If there are no such actions pending, I will call the captain of the watch and inform him that he is to proceed with his preparations. At that point the inmate will be moved from the holding area to the execution chamber."

Gordon was suddenly aware that someone had actually dared to utter the word "execution" for the first time. Until now, he had only heard the more ambiguous "proceedings."

"When the inmate has been situated, the captain of the watch will notify me and I in turn will inform Assistant Warden Earnhardt, who will then accompany you to the witness area."

The warden paused and Gordon noticed that he had shifted his eyeline. His focus was now on a point somewhere behind the witnesses, the "point in space" that actors in the theater play to. The change was subtle, but Gordon sensed it was crucial. The Noise reached a new crescendo.

"When you enter the witness area, the first thing you will see is the inmate. He will be strapped to the gurney and the IVs will already be set. His head will be left free so he can turn to see you and the witnesses in the other witness room. The family members will be allowed to enter first, followed by the press and two correctional officers. You will then be locked in the witness area until the proceedings are completed."

Gordon's heart slammed against the inside of his chest. The idea of being locked in had never occurred to him. In his worst anticipatory nightmares there had never been a point of no return. The Noise grew louder and louder until he was only aware that the warden was still speaking because his lips were still moving.

"The inmate will then be allowed to make a statement.

When he is finished, I will give the signal to begin. The first drug that will be administered is pentobarbital, just like you would be given for a major surgery in the hospital. It will render the inmate unconscious in about three or four seconds. Now, when the pentobarbital is administered, every inmate reacts differently. Sometimes they will yawn. Sometimes you will hear a groan. Some will even snore. They're all different. The next drug administered is called pancurium bromide. This will stop the inmate's breathing. The last drug is potassium chloride, which stops the heart. Administering the drugs will take less than two minutes. I will then wait for five minutes and at the end of that time I will ask the doctor to step in and examine the inmate. The doctor will then pronounce death and note the time."

The warden took two crablike steps to his left and two large correctional officers stepped into the gap created between himself and Earnhardt. They wore the uniform of the prison's tactical unit — long-sleeved khaki shirts with epaulets, pressed to a military crispness and stretched tight across overpumped biceps, with matching pants tucked into the tops of black canvas combat boots. Larkin resumed eye contact with his audience.

"These gentleman are Officers Mabry and Newsome. They will accompany you to the witness area. Their primary function is to ensure that no one attempts to interfere with these proceedings here tonight. If anyone should become unruly or otherwise behave in an unseemly manner, these officers are authorized, at their own discretion, to remove them from the witness area. You will be separated from the inmate by a Plexiglas window. He will be able to see you. You will be able to hear him as he makes his statement by means of a microphone near his head. He will not be able to hear you. Should anyone shout or become abusive, he or she will be removed. Should anyone strike or bang on the window, he or she will be removed."

The warden went on down his customary list of offenses punishable by removal and then suddenly the military demeanor dissolved and was replaced once again by the familiar funeral director's smile and barely audible monotone.

"We have a job to do here today. That is to enforce the letter of the law and the will of the people of this state. With your cooperation we will accomplish that task as quickly and as painlessly as possible. Thank you for your attention."

Warden Larkin turned and exited the room, followed by Earnhardt and Chaplain Meeks, leaving the two massive guards standing like sphinxes on either side of the door.

The witnesses sat in silence, some of them occasionally checking the clock on the wall above the door. Midnight came and went. By 12:15 there was still no word and the suspense was starting to get to Gordon.

When he closed his eyes he saw Andy Camacho on his knees, head bowed, and eyes closed in penitence, being led in the rosary by Father Ramirez. He was wearing prison whites, the shirt open at the neck, a silver medal gleaming against his dark skin, and it seemed to move with every pulse of a heart that was beating out its last few hundred repetitions. He resembled an oil painting of a revolutionary hero, a courageous peasant martyred in some righteous, romantic cause. There was a bare light bulb behind him, obscured by his head, and the light surrounded him like a halo. Gordon shook himself but not hard enough. Now he was flat on his back and Warden Larkin and

Chaplain Meeks stood over *him*. He tried to move, but when he did he was held fast by thick, stiff leather straps. "No! No!"

He shuddered, violently it seemed to him, but no one else in the waiting area noticed. He was relieved to find that he hadn't really shouted out loud after all. He wondered what was taking so long.

The delay was a "little emergency" in the other waiting area. David Price, the court-appointed lawyer, had gotten up to go to the restroom and had made all of three steps in that direction before falling face down on the hard vinyl-over-concrete floor, sustaining a nasty cut on his chin and a mild concussion. Now Camacho had only two witnesses.

Meanwhile, Gordon was beginning to calm down. The Noise was still there, though somewhat quieted now, or maybe he had simply become accustomed to it. He had come this far and there was no turning back now, in any case. He wondered if anyone noticed that he had been struggling to keep his composure. He needn't have. Outwardly, Gordon Elliot appeared as placid and opaque as lake water.

It was 12:50 before they saw Earnhardt again. He was alone this time.

"Follow me, please, family first."

The Noise in Gordon's ears swelled to a roar. Lieutenant Abraham helped him to his feet and steadied him as he took that first excruciating step. As they moved toward the door, District Attorney Boquist fell into step behind them, followed by Russ McBride and Lorrie White, with the two tactical officers bringing up the rear. They turned right following a hallway lined with offices, some dark, some lit, their doors standing open and their occupants looking busy at their desks. It seemed to Gordon that each bureaucrat they passed stopped whatever he or she was doing and attempted to engage him as he passed.

They intersected another hallway and turned right, and then right again, arriving at another double door in the rear of the visitors' center. The guard stationed there nodded at Gordon, who stared blankly back.

They followed a covered sidewalk in a straight line across the compound. The state had built the aluminum awning to protect the witnesses from the elements as they crossed between the visitors' center and the Death House, but tonight it was unnecessary. The first minutes of Andres Camacho's last day on earth were cool and dry, a crescent moon hanging low over the penitentiary, like a great golden cradle. At the end of the sidewalk there were two open doors about eight feet apart. The light emanating from inside the low, monolithic brick building was amplified by the surrounding darkness. Guards stood waiting, keys in hand, by either door. The group was directed to the door on the left. Earnhardt sidestepped, allowing Gordon to enter first. He was about to cross the threshold when the guard beside the door locked eyes with him for an instant. Gordon fought back the panic rising in his throat like bile and stepped, finally and irreversibly it seemed, through the door.

Just as promised, the first thing he saw was Andres Camacho lying on a specially built hospital gurney with armrests projecting from either side at forty-five-degree angles. He was secured by means of five broad leather straps across his legs and torso. Four smaller straps held his arms, which were wrapped in Ace bandages, the kind used to bind sprained ankles. Gordon followed the IV lines from where they emerged from the folds of the bandages, threading through a series of metal loops, before disappearing through the stump of a PVC tube into the wall. Just above the tube there was a small, mirrored glass window. Gordon caught a faint silhouette as it moved, wraithlike behind the window — the executioner settling into his station.

The witness area was the size of a smallish walk-in closet. There was barely room for Gordon, Lieutenant Abraham, and DA Boquist to stand shoulder to shoulder in the first row, nearest the glass. Gordon could hear Russ McBride and Lorrie White scribbling away on their little pads, the door closing behind them, and then the dull "clack" of the tumbler as the key turned in the lock.

Camacho turned his head, with obvious difficulty, to look at Gordon through the glass. The victim's witnesses were in the room nearest his head, and he had to twist his neck in an awkward fashion, distorting his features. Gordon thought he looked helpless, like a child or an animal caught in a fiendish trap that only humans could devise. He stood there impaled on Camacho's piercing gaze, with the Noise and his own heartbeat competing for his attention, until he was finally rescued by the sound of the door opening in the adjoining witness area. Camacho turned his attention to the arrival of "his" witnesses in the other room.

Warden Larkin stood nearest Camacho's head, but kept as much distance as space permitted, about five feet. At the other end of the gurney Chaplain Meeks stationed himself much closer, almost brushing Camacho's leg with his hip. Gordon jumped when the loudspeaker, mounted on the ceiling above his head, suddenly crackled to life. It was Warden Larkin speaking.

"Do you have anything to say?"

Camacho raised his head as far as he was able and after acknowledging his witnesses, twisted his head around once again to confront Gordon.

"Yo be inocente." Then, to everyone's surprise, he translated for himself. "I am innocent."

He mercifully turned away. Staring straight up at the ceiling, he took a long ragged breath, closed his eyes, and began saying a Hail Mary in Spanish. Gordon noticed that Chaplain Meeks was resting his right hand on Camacho's leg just below the knee. For some reason that he couldn't explain, the contact offended him. Now more than ever Gordon wanted the whole horrible business over with. Finished.

What Gordon didn't know was that the Hail Mary was the signal that Camacho had agreed to so that Warden Larkin knew he was ready, and Gordon had missed the warden's subtle hand signal to the unseen executioner behind the one-way glass. Therefore he had no way of knowing that the poison had already made its way down the plastic tubing and was racing through Andres Camacho's body.

". . . ahora y en la hora de la muerte nuestra . . ."

Andy's prayer was interrupted by a sound from his own lips, a low-pitched bark, a startling, incongruous sound, like a small child with whooping cough, as the air was suddenly forced from his lungs and his head pitched forward until his chin lodged on his chest. It was as if an invisible anvil had been dropped on his chest from a great height. It was much more violent than Gordon had ever imagined it would be. He had convinced himself that this would be different somehow. On paper it was efficient and clinical. Instead, there was the unmistakable sense that he was witnessing a soul being brutally and unnaturally ripped from a human body.

Andres Camacho's chest heaved a couple more times and

there was a soft hissing sound like air leaking from a punctured tire. Then he lay still, eyes fixed, mouth open. It was obvious to everyone present, rookies and veterans alike, that the man was dead, but the protocol had not yet been satisfied. One minute passed. Then two. Once in a while the warden checked his watch. Every minute seemed to pass more slowly than the one before. Gordon stood transfixed, unable to look away no matter how badly he wanted to, his heart pounding and the reporters scribbling and the Noise roaring . . . and then the door opened as the warden motioned for the doctor to come in.

The doctor was an ancient, angular man in a well-worn dark suit, and his whole manner stated that he'd performed his duties many, many times before. He shined a small flashlight into Camacho's frozen eyes, first one then the other. A pale, bony finger along the side of the neck told the old man what he already knew, but he continued with his examination anyway. Finally, using an antique stethoscope given to him by his father, also a physician, when he graduated from medical school, he listened for a heartbeat that he knew he would not find. When he was satisfied, he straightened up, checked his watch, and on his way out of the room, as if it were an afterthought, noted the time: 1:14.

Someone in the back of the room knocked on the door. Three sharp, even raps, like a kid's clubhouse code and then the key in the lock. When the door was opened, the night air rushed in to fill the vacuum that death creates.

"Family first, please."

That meant Gordon. He must have stumbled as he turned around to leave, because Lieutenant Abraham was there, as always, to catch him. The rest of the witnesses flattened themselves against the wall as best they could to allow him to pass, so he had to face each one — Boquist, Russ McBride, Lorrie

White, Mabry, and Newsome — he ran the gauntlet. When he reached the end and stepped out into the fresh air, he took a deep breath, in through his nose and out through his mouth. He noticed that something had changed. Something was missing. The moon was still there, only a few degrees lower in the eastern sky. Soon it would disappear behind the Segregation Building and then dip closer and closer to the horizon until it was lost, even to the free world. His heart rate was settling down a bit, and . . . *That's it! The Noise! The goddamn infernal Noise!* For the first time since he entered the prison, a little more than three hours ago, it had finally, mercifully stopped.

The witnesses filed back into the visitors' center in the same order that they had left. Turned right, then left, then left again, and they were back in the lounge — except for McBride and White. They had left the entourage, unnoticed, sometime after the group entered the building. As usual, they had joined the rest of their colleagues in the breezeway in front of the visitors' center where the microphones and cameras were being set up in anticipation of a statement from Gordon Elliot. But it was not to be.

While the press was busy setting up and checking their hardware, Assistant Warden Allen Earnhardt, along with Officers Mabry and Newsome, escorted Gordon Elliot through the back door, along the inside of the wire, to a service gate on the east side of the prison. Until that night the east gate had only been used to facilitate the coming and going of the hearse from the local funeral parlor. Tonight Gordon Elliot and Andres Camacho would leave the institution by the same route.

When Earnhardt asked if Gordon would like to make a statement to the press, the answer was an emphatic "No."

Earnhardt was more than a little surprised. This was certainly unprecedented. There was always at least one member of the victim's family who hadn't had enough "closure," and the state was more than willing to accommodate them. They were always permitted to stand there, attempting in vain to soothe their pain and rage with their own noxious venom, while the cameras whirred and clicked and the microphones bore silent witness. And then they would leave, still hurting, still angry and secretly feeling betrayed because the system's ultimate remedy had brought them no peace.

While there was no precedent for a hasty departure by a witness from the institution, there was a contingency. Gordon was ushered into a waiting van and driven around the perimeter "dogtrot" and dropped at his car before anyone was the wiser. Earnhardt had said his goodbyes at the gate. The driver of the van, an officer Gordon hadn't seen before, waited for him to find his keys and fumble for the lock. As soon as Gordon was in his car, the van pulled away. For a moment Gordon sat there, staring at the eerily lit compound, unable to grasp the fact that it was really over. He had walked right into the mouth of the Beast and emerged unscathed. Now all he had to do was drive.

And drive he did, past the checkpoints, stopping only at the last guard shack long enough to pop his hood and his trunk for the guard and then back out on the blacktop, and through the wasteland. He fought an overwhelming impulse to floor the accelerator for the entire six miles back to the interstate. Then he urged the big Lincoln down the on-ramp and smoothly out into the sparse traffic.

He checked his mirrors, temporarily readjusting his rearview and turning on his interior lights to look briefly into his own eyes. Bad idea. He readjusted the mirror and got back down to the business at hand, which was simply to drive. His suitcase was in the trunk. His passport and ticket were in the outside pocket, and for the first time it began to sink in.

He made it. They didn't know, after all.

They didn't know that when Andres Camacho had proclaimed his innocence, less than a minute before leaving this world, he was telling the truth. That he wasn't lying when he testified that while Joan Elliot was being raped and strangled to death that night twelve years ago, he was sound asleep in his little apartment above the garage, dreaming of the first sweet days of the rainy season in his village in El Salvador. That he had panicked when he awoke the next morning and found Joan's broken body lying on the bedroom floor naked from the waist down. That, terrified that he would be blamed for the horror he had discovered, he had taken the only vehicle available and fled, instinctively south, toward Salvador. Toward the home he would never see again.

They also didn't know that when the state police contacted Gordon Elliot at his cabin at the lake, he had lied about being out there all weekend alone. That actually he had spent Friday night there, with his mistress of two years, a twenty-seven-year-old associate at the firm named Sandy Hilliard. They didn't know that he had left in the early hours of Saturday morning, telling Sandy that he was finally going to ask Joan for a divorce, so that they could be married. That leaving his car in the long-term parking lot at the airport, he had taken the shuttle to the terminal and rented a dark blue Ford Taurus and then driven home. That he had parked around the corner from his house and wearing a black ski mask and cotton gloves, approached his own home from the alley, entering through the back gate and literally creeping past the guesthouse where Andres Camacho slept. That after carefully making his way through Andy's lovingly tended garden, he had used his key to let himself in through the French doors that opened onto the patio.

From there it was only a dozen halting steps to his and Joan's bedroom. He had stood over her watching her sleep for a moment, her face half lit by a rectangular patch of light emanating from the bathroom door, which had been left open as a night-light, creating an eerie film noir effect. Only her eyes were visible, which made it that much more startling when she suddenly opened them and began to scream. Gordon panicked, dropping the pistol he had planned to use to murder his wife of twenty-three years, and fell on her with his bare hands like an animal. He seized her by the throat and lifted her up out of bed, high enough that her feet kicked in the air like a hanged man's and then he squeezed, harder and harder, until he heard her larynx collapse with a sickening, wet snap. When she voided and went limp, like a broken doll in his arms, he lowered her gently to the floor and left her to lie in a puddle of her own urine. He picked up the pistol and tucked it into the waistband of his pants, removed Joan's panties and left them lying in the middle of the floor, and left the way he came, breaking a window in one of the French doors on his way out.

Arriving on the scene early the next afternoon, Lieutenant Roscoe Abraham saw the half-naked body when he was barely through the door and immediately assumed he was dealing with a sex crime. He never looked back. He knew that Gordon had no history of domestic violence. He also knew that Gordon was an attorney and that as a member of that fraternity he would be tough to prosecute. He could hear the DA laughing his ass off now. When it was discovered that both Joan's car and the Salvadoran gardener were missing, Abraham was relieved. He was getting too old for tabloid cases. But there was a lot that Abraham didn't know as well.

He didn't know that Gordon Elliot was a degenerate gambler. No one did, because Gordon was a firm believer in not shitting in his own backyard. In Gordon's circle of friends and associates, appearances were everything. No one really cared how you got your jollies — dope, girls, even boys — as long as you didn't get caught and bring scandal to the firm's doorstep.

So Gordon did his gambling in Las Vegas. He always went alone, he always bet big and he always lost, and for years he was always good for it. That is until one particularly bad run of luck left him with a stack of unpaid markers all over town. As was the custom, one of the Vegas boys bought up all of Gordon's bad paper and threatened to notify his partners in the law firm if he didn't pay up. All of Gordon's legitimate lines of credit were tapped out. As a stopgap measure he emptied a client's escrow account of a little more than a million dollars. His credit in Vegas restored, he continued to gamble hoping against hope to get well. He was flying home from Vegas on a redeye one night after losing $250,000 in one long weekend, when he remembered that he and Joan held two million dollars in insurance on each other's lives. The policies were more than twenty years old, as they had been purchased right after they were married. If something were to happen to Joan, he could collect the benefit on her policy and, since Joan was the sole beneficiary, cash in the premiums on his. The net would be over three million dollars.

Gordon reached the airport exit an hour before his scheduled flight time. Cancun. That's what the tickets said. That's where Sandy had always wanted to go.

Poor Sandy. She had hung in there all those years. She had stood right by his side waiting patiently for this day. The day that the whole nightmare would finally end and she and Gordon could go away for a long, much deserved vacation. She had kept up appearances for years until Gordon decided that the time was right. She had been prepared to lie for him when he returned to the cabin that night and told her that he had found his wife murdered, but it never came up. He said that he had panicked and run and now he was afraid the police would suspect him, and she believed every word. She had even put up with Gordon's gambling. She had done well at the firm and she was a partner now with a practice of her own, and they always managed to cover his losses somehow. She had always believed that she and Gordon would be married once this ugly mess was over. Maybe then she would see the old Gordon again. Things had never really gotten back to normal in all those years since Joan's murder, and maybe this end of Andy Camacho's life would be the beginning of a new life for Gordon and Sandy.

Of course, Sandy didn't know that the man she loved was a murderer and a liar, and now she was at the bottom of the lake about three miles from Gordon's cabin, shot through the head.

Gordon didn't get off at the airport exit. He just kept driving. He didn't really know why. Suddenly, he just didn't feel much like Mexico. Or maybe it was the idea of leaving the safety of the big Lincoln. All that steel around him was somehow reassuring, along with that soft, humming sound that radial tires make on dry pavement, when they're nice and warm and really hooked up to the highway. That was just what he needed. That and some time alone. Time to sort out the way he was feeling right now. He knew this feeling. He had felt it before. In fact, he had carried it around with him for the past twelve years. At first it had manifested itself as sheer terror, but over the years his fear had moderated until, in time, he had become perversely exhilarated by the idea that at any moment Roscoe Abraham could come knocking on his door with a warrant for his arrest.

Everything was different now. It was still a dark, hollow, lonely feeling but it had become familiar, and he was no longer threatened by it. Especially now that no one would ever know that Andres Camacho had paid with his life for a crime that he didn't commit and that Gordon Elliot, the only man on earth who could save him, had stood by and watched and didn't say a word. And it felt exactly the same as it did twelve years ago when he killed Joan and last night when he shot Sandy using a pillow to muffle the sound and deflect the flying skull fragments and pieces of her brain. It felt like murder. And like everything else, it got a little easier every time.

A WELL-TEMPERED HEART

THE FIRST TIME he saw her he loved her. Even then, as he resolved to press his suit for her, he was painfully aware from experience on both sides of the battlefield that he was utterly defenseless. He was habitually reckless in affairs of the heart, so he wasn't surprised at how easily he fell, only that he loved her selflessly and without condition. The very idea that he, in his middle years and after all he had been through, could love someone with all his heart and soul, expecting and probably receiving nothing in return, was at once terrifying and exhilarating. It was the Great Love that he had aspired to all of his life and he was not about to miss it, for if ever a Romantic walked this earth it was he.

He had entered into every relationship in his life in good faith, reveling in the breathless flush of new love for as long as it lasted and then valiantly pretending not to notice that it had faded for as long as he could. When he finally moved on, he always left something of him behind and took something of her along until he became, in essence, every lover he had ever been with. He assimilated all of their strengths and weaknesses, and any virtue he possessed was learned from one woman or another, a consolation prize bestowed on him at their parting. Even his fears were an amalgam of theirs, transmitted through dreams, he suspected, as they lay in each other's arms. But fear neither made nor broke him, for fear after all is a function of the mind and he was by and large a creature of the heart, adherent to a loftier agenda. Although there was nothing in his experience that would recommend love as a viable course of action, he forged ahead blindly trusting that if he stayed the course, he was destined for a transcendent love one day. Each time the net result was more or less the same, another painful memory, a wound that he allowed to bleed freely, knowing that it was the healing rather than the hurting that left the scar. This partition that he had meticulously crafted between faith and reason served him as a rampart against callousness, until the day that he saw her and knew her and set out to win her, his eyes wide open and possessed of a well-tempered heart.

She came to him shrouded in layer upon layer of mystery — seven veils at least, each denser than the one before. He had never been a patient man but loving her demanded it, so patience was the order of the day. He waited and watched and listened and learned, determined to know everything about her. Although he ached to touch her, he learned the value of distance, standing only near enough that she always knew he was there if she needed him. They rarely spoke, except when he traveled, when using the miles between them as a safety net, they ran up embarrassing phone bills. Even then, they circled any discussion of the feeling between them like moths around a candle, somehow managing to pull out just before their wings went up in flames. When she was near, he could only watch in rapt fascination when she triumphed and in silent anguish when she stumbled. She stumbled often, sometimes into the arms of another, and having gained her confidence, he was subjected to all of the gory details. He believed, at times, that his fearless heart had finally met its match, but it only grew stronger, enabling him to love her more — and better — with every passing day.

Their first kisses were stolen ones, occasional lapses during ostensibly innocent rendezvous on neutral ground, after which they returned to their respective lives and tried to pretend that nothing had happened. Then, in the spring following a hopeful summer, a melancholy autumn, and a cold, lonely but resolute winter, he finally held her in his arms. When they made love for the first time, he thought that he would surely die, for he knew of nothing in this life that could compare to the softness of her skin and the music of her voice in his ear. That night she fell asleep instantly, her head resting on his heaving chest while the pounding within kept him awake for hours, measuring out a steady cadence and reminding him that this was but a battle joined and that a long campaign lay ahead. He set out to follow her through her dreams.

He gave himself completely, holding no part of his heart in reserve, knowing full well that she could only give in return that which she possessed. She had lost much of herself in ten empty years and only time and love could make her whole again. Her curiosity about his past was insatiable, and he told her things he had never told anyone. Her past was of little interest to him, but when she spoke of it he listened attentively, because he knew she needed to give her dark days voice in order to exorcise them. She reciprocated with every healing touch of her hand, and even the physical marks of his former life faded in time, not overnight, but gradually giving way to love and care.

Their life together was filled with bright mornings and starlit nights that consistently outshone the darker times between. Even those hard days were times of learning when their differences became gifts from one to the other. By example he taught her courage and tenacity. She offered tolerance and compassion in kind, and they both learned their lessons well, if by rote. Then, one day, he looked up and saw her through clear, new eyes, unclouded by passion or need and found her standing straight and tall and strong without his assistance, and he loved her more than ever.

One night he was awakened by a dissonance in his dreams to an empty space beside him in their bed. He found her in the garden, and though she'd finished crying hours before, the moonlight betrayed a trail of tears across her cheek. He started to ask what the matter was then thought better of it, for he already knew the answer. In all her life, she had never been truly on her own. Her dreams had been stolen from her by circumstance when she was not much more than a child, and she had responded by simply resolving to no longer dream. Now that that path lay open to her again, at long last, he knew that nothing he could say or do would keep her from her journey. He'd always known that a day might come when loving her the best he could would mean letting her go, and now that it was here he was not about to sully the moment or the memory of their time together. So he simply said "I love you" and "goodbye."

And even then his trusty heart refused to break. Any wound or lesion it had borne before their meeting had long since faded into distant memory until it beat steady and true as the day that he was born, fortified somehow by the certainty that it had already survived the hardest blow that life could deal it. Years later, on the day that he died, his heart never once fluttered or faltered but simply stopped between one beat and the next as he closed his eyes and remembered how beautiful she was the first time he saw her.